Pippin Pearmain is filming a part in an indie film while also attending a music festival and working on her ballet, *Delphine*. Mysteries surround her, but she hasn't much time to sort them out. She has the offer of a puppy, a reunion with an old friend, a new agent to deal with, and a new plan for a family heirloom. With all this going on, she still has to consider her dwindling family, her very strange cats, and what, if anything, is going to change in her future.

A few weeks ago, her cottage, the cats, and her bucket list were enough. Now she's making a comeback, but where will it take her? She can go home to her reclusive existence, but there's so much more to life than wrestling with cranky lemon trees. Pip thinks she might be up to it, but what if she's wrong? Yet . . . not so long ago she went overboard from the yacht *Tulpenmanie*. She survived the Experience and thrived in the aftermath, so maybe the challenges ahead will be navigable after all.

Performing Pippin Pearmain 6

ISBN: 978-1-4874-3719-0
Cover art by Martine Jardin

Published by eXtasy Books Inc

Look for us online at:
www.eXtasybooks.com

Performing Pippin Pearmain 6

By

Lark Westerly

Dedication

For everyone whose life has been disturbed, and who has carried on and been magnificent . . . well, sort of.

Author's Note

Fiction and Reality

Major places in the story, such as Tasmania, the city of Sydney and the state of Victoria do exist. So does Bass Strait. The towns of Jellico Bay and Delmsford are made up, as is Delphinium Island. The suburb of Windhill is made up. If it existed, it would be somewhere near North Sydney. The suburb of Glebe is real as is the iconic Sydney Harbour Bridge.

Pip's story covers a year, taking her from her reclusive cottage in Jellico Bay to her old hometown of Delmsford, to the magical fossmere, on to Sydney and thence to Delphinium Island. The nine books compile into one continuing story, slowly revealing the mystery and magic that has been part of Pip's world all along.

And how did I come to write Pip's story? It all began with a flower show . . . and with a bucket.

The story so far . . .

Book One

Introducing Pippin Pearmain—small, eccentric, determined, sixty-six, and ruled by cats. Until a decade ago, Pip earned her living by playing offbeat roles on stage and screen, but after her mother and her agent died in the same week, parts dried up and she moved to Jellico Bay. During a visit to her old hometown she encountered her cousins, Lupin de Leon and Juniper "Jan" Sharman. They, and Jan's daughter, Clarkia, were the only remaining members of the Laurel-Pearmain-de-Leon family. Over afternoon tea at the Delmsford

Flower Show, Pip revealed her long-held secret—her bucket list—a literal list of interesting buckets. In return, her cousins wrote down their secrets.

Home in her cottage with the original cat and the back-up cat, who communicate with her in what she thinks of as Cat-Morse, Pip read the secrets. Jan revealed herself as the novelist Juniper Gin. Lupin's secret was shocking—she had just a few months to live.

After Lupin's passing, Jan met the cats Kittisack and Amberjill and received a bucket Pip had promised her for Lupin's last repose. They discussed the provenance of a family heirloom—two copies of a book called *Grandmother's Sunshine.* Lacking heirs, Pip had once offered her copy to a young friend, whose mother refused to let her accept it. A call from Jan's daughter prompted Jan to dash off, leaving Pip with Lupin's legacy—an envelope and a pottery cat.

Book Two

Pip received a call from Magda Saxer, announcing herself as Pip's new agent and offering a role in a film called *Half-Life of the Lost*. The cats were unexpectedly in favour. They suggested Jan's daughter would come to look after them.

Lupin's envelope contained a voucher written in disappearing ink. Pip called the information line, whereupon Gerry Trip, Lupin's ex-colleague at Vouch-Safe, informed her she had one hour to prepare for a mystery Experience.

Gerry's step-grandson, Jamie, promised to cat-sit. He drove Pip to a rendezvous.

Pip boarded the yacht *Tulpenmanie,* crewed by pleasant Zach, his odd girlfriend, Jisinia, and Jamie's uncle, Tane.

When Pip realised Tane was missing, she called triple zero. Jisinia confiscated the phone but returned it. Pip rationalised that Tane must have returned to shore.

That night, Tane, who was a silversmith, came back. After resizing a ring for her, he invited Pip to meet his family. She agreed.

Tane picked her up and jumped into the sea.

Book Three

Tane took Pip through an underwater gateway to *over there* where she spent a week with his extended family, practising ballet with Jane and making friends with Tane's spouse, Jillian Jules. The fossmere, a waterfall pool, delighted Pip. She left her tektite ring in the cave behind the falls in gratitude for her adventure. Tane and Jules took her to Hob's Island where she added a new bucket to her list. A sighting of dolphins gave her the idea for a ballet.

Back at Lemonwood Cottage, Pip discovered Jamie, her driver, was a "mutie" or *mutable fay*. He had a second self—a dog he called Kakao.

Jan asked if her daughter Clarkia might come to stay at Lemonwood Cottage while Pip had her screen test.

Book Four

Pip met her agent, Magda, at Sydney airport. Magda's friend, Pandora, drove them to a guesthouse run by Edgar and Joan Treadwell. Next morning, Edgar took Pip to a grassy area *over there* to do her ballet practice.

Pip went with Magda to Diamond Spellman Studio for a screen test where she met the film crew . . . and also Matin Campania, from Arts in Tune, the company co-producing the film.

The filming was to be part of a dance festival. Pip looked forward to researching music for her dolphin ballet.

On the way back from the screen test, Pip visited the Fairy Gardens, where she saw sculpted statues of the founders. She decided to commission the sculptor to make her a bucket. He was away, so Pip left a message with the alarming Frances le Fay.

Pip borrowed an encyclopaedia called *Orders of the Fay* from Edgar and also ordered a set from Jonquil Orange of *The Orange Grove* bookshop. On a whim, she enquired about

Grandmother's Sunshine. Jonquil believed it was a myth but said someone else had asked for it recently. Pip prevaricated, unwilling to admit her family had two copies of such a rare title.

After a return to the fossmere to dance with Jane and work on her dolphin ballet, *Delphine,* Pip went to the Fairy Gardens to finish blocking the ballet. There, she met the Dames with Dogs. Her attempt to use Cat-Morse on the dogs failed. She spotted a mutie . . . a young man with a Scottie dog self. She tried Dog-Morse on an uncooperative black spaniel who was revealed to be Gillan, the mutie's mother. From her time at the fossmere, Pip identified Gillan and her sons as piskies.

Gillan recognised Pip from her role in the cult film *The House of Heriot,* in which she had starred with Alain Barfleur. Finding Gillan hard work, Pip left, but Gillan made her a remarkable offer.

Book Five

Pip tried and failed to take herself *over there* without a pilot. She then travelled to Delphinium Island with Magda in Matin Campania's van. Magda asked for details about *Grandmother's Sunshine.* Matin distracted her, to Pip's relief.

At the island, they met Gillan's son Mull St Ives. Pip and Magda were assigned a cabin. Pip went to the Icehouse market for an official shirt, where she met Jessie and Asher, two elves, and encountered Tane Pendennis from *Tulpenmanie* and the fossmere.

Pip joined other dancers and musicians to Dance in the Dawn, and saw Matin's wife, Tamzin Campania, playing her fiddle. She did ballet practice with Tane's daughter Jane, who had arrived with her cousin, Jamie's sister Laura. Jane had found principal dancers for Pip's ballet.

Pip met Costas Capricorn who played impromptu music for her ballet rehearsal.

Filming began for *Half-Life of the Lost.* Pip met the actors, members of a company called Biblio-Rep, the crew from

Diamond Spellman Studio, eccentric wardrobe master, Ward, and Humphry "Humph" Carpenter-Rivers, the playwright, who had invented a new prologue for two people and a horse.

With the prologue in the can, Pip filmed the first scene with Star Calder-Quince, who played comatose Perdita.

During the break, Pip headed to the barn where she met Tamzin again. She was started to see the drawing Tamzin was working on . . . a copy of a picture in *Grandmother's Sunshine*.

Pip learned that she and Tamzin had known one another twenty-five years before. Tamzin had been her little friend, Angie Blake, who had lived for a while in Pip's hometown in Tasmania. They arranged to meet the next morning to discuss ballet music . . . and Pip hatched a new plan.

Book Six, the one you are about to read, begins on Delphinium Island part-way through making the film . . .

The story continues . . .

CHAPTER ONE. SORTING CHAOS

Pippin Picotee Pearmain should have slept poorly on her second night on Delphinium Island. She'd spent a packed day among new acquaintances and debriefed with one old friend she hadn't seen in twenty-five years.

Her brain fizzed with new information, ideas, possibilities, and the nervous feeling that came from juggling too many mental apples and trying not to drop any on her neat and serviceable toes.

Knowing she had a snowball's chance in a hot bath of getting any sleep while her mind was rampaging up, down, and around like a wasp in a bottle, Pip decided to make a list to sort the chaos into order. She loved lists. They were soothing.

After a chaotic supper with her agent and the cheerful and talkative cast of *Half-Life of the Lost,* she retreated to cabin six, where she and Magda were living for the duration of the festival.

Magda, being more gregarious and more inclined for networking than Pip was, stayed out to schmooze with—someone or other. Pip didn't much care who it was and didn't bother to enquire. She trusted her agent would be happily occupied for at least an hour while she wound down and generally stabilised her mind.

In cabin six, and finally alone, Pip put the kettle on and laid out the caddy of camomile tea she'd brought from home beside a personalised teacup, unexpectedly provided by Dance in Tune. It was wreathed in music notes with the festival logo and a green star outline with a streaky apple inside. Pip loved it all the more when she turned it upside down and found the maker's mark—the familiar be-smocked hob man with a giant ear of corn. Faintly discernible beneath it was the monogram *AC*.

Ardal Cornfellow.

Knowing the potter, or at least the painter, was her friend Jane's beau who had taken her riding gave the cup added value to Pip.

While the tea steeped, she stood in the centre of the cabin, waiting for her ears to stop zinging from all the chatter, music, and laughter of a dance festival. It was wonderful, but also daunting for someone who lived in a cottage by the sea with three cats—one of which was made of pottery—a terrifying lemon tree, a sly gooseberry bush, a lot of still-packed boxes and crates, and a placid, blue-tongued lizard.

When her heartrate settled, she did a few pliés to quieten her mind. Then she poured her tea and took her feint-ruled pad and green pen out of her messenger bag.

She settled on the bed with the tea on a table beside her, paged through her list of beautiful buckets, past secrets written down by her cousins Lupin and Jan, and by Zach Rowan, who crewed the yacht *Tulpenmanie*. She paged beyond the work she'd done on three separate ballets, and on past a list of pros and cons she'd written down regarding the offer of a puppy from Gillan St Ives.

She had the new Treadwell bucket to add to her list, but she decided to leave that until tomorrow, or maybe even next week when her mind was less busy.

Having finally reached a clear page, she admired it briefly. She knew some people found blank pages daunting, but she never had. Blank pages were like holidays to her—full of opportunities and potential wonder. Unless they were shopping lists, of course. Pip rarely bothered with those, because she always bought the same range of provisions from Jellico Bay

Essentials. She could trolley-up her regular provisions in fifteen minutes—providing Mister Essentials had been good enough to leave his aisles alone. Every now and again he got spring fever, winter woes, summer scrambles, or autumn annoyance and shifted the contents of aisle nine somewhere else. Pip didn't approve of that because it bothered her routine.

She took up her green ink pen and wrote *Things to Do* in her tiny script.

It was her habit to start writing her lists immediately, but this time she waited for a few seconds to see what item on her agenda might pop up first.

No point in putting them down in order of importance . . . and no need to consider must-do, want-to-do and urgent-or-not.

She wrote down a number one and, after a little more thought, she wrote down *Family.*

Might as well get it over with.

She breathed in and added, slowly, Regarding the Laurel-Pearmain-de-Leon Family.

Extant members.

Pippin Picotee Pearmain. Me. Myself.

She felt awkward at putting her name down at the head of the list, but she was the eldest of them now, and so might be considered the head of the family by herself if not by the others.

She added her age—sixty-six. Then she filled in a few more facts. Performer. Single. Lives in Lemonwood Cottage, Jellico Bay, Tasmania, with three cats. Temporarily working on a film—*Half-Life of the Lost*—at the Dance in Tune festival on Delphinium Island. First formal job in eleven years. It feels both familiar and peculiar. Just like life, I suppose.

The second name had to be Cousin Jan's.

Juniper "Jan" Sharman nee de Leon. Sixty-four. Author, known as Juniper Gin. I think this role is comparatively recent. Must ask her when and why and how it came about.

Married to Mark Sharman since the late 1970s. She married him the year I was working on *Ruby Shoes Emporium.* Lives—

Her pen hovered uncertainly. She realised with shame that she didn't know Jan's current address, save that it was somewhere in northern Tasmania. Nor was she absolutely sure that Jan was still married to Mark, or indeed at all. Until a chance meeting at the Delmsford Flower Show in February, they'd not been in contact for ten years. Jan had mentioned her husband once or twice, but not with enough context for Pip to know whether he was still living with her. She *had* seen Jan twisting her wedding ring, and Jan *had* mentioned something about betrayal. Could that have referred to trouble *chez* Sharman, or might she have been talking about something else?

Pip shrugged. The entry would have to do.

Number three was Clarkia Sharman. Thirty-seven . . . I think. Jan's daughter with Mark. Single. Lived in southern Tasmania with a perfidious partner until recently—though as soon as she discovered his perfidy she left. Currently staying at Lemonwood Cottage and minding the cats.

Pip glanced over the three names and sighed heavily. That was it. All that was left of the Laurel-Pearmain-de-Leon family, and *she* was the only one who bore any of the original surnames. As far as she knew, the Laurels and de Leons of their branch were extinct.

Just us. No other cousins.

How on earth did that happen? Maybe—possibly—people from small families were drawn to one another. Little Mum and Aunt Helen had been twins, but Little Dad and Uncle Lance de Leon were only children. Pip had a vague memory of being told Little Dad had once had a brother, but that he'd died young . . . or something. It might have been before Little Dad was born. Just one of those things no one really spoke of in detail. She supposed she could find out through official channels, but why bother? It wouldn't bring him back.

But I might have had an uncle. I wonder what his name was.

She considered other apple names. They'd have to be old ones that were familiar in 1920. Bramley, perhaps.

Uncle Bram.

She stopped short. Grandad Laurel's first name was Bram. She'd assumed it was short for Abraham, but what if he'd been christened Bramley?

Stop that, she told herself sharply.

She wrote a new heading and recorded past members of her family, known and unknown, adding a few details she'd got from Jan as well as a progression she had worked out with Magda. Though why Magda cared about Pip's family tree was still mostly unexplained. They were not related.

Past Members.

Generation one. Grandmother Aster. Surname? No idea. Lived? No clue where, or even when. All I know is that she had two granddaughters named Cammie and Callie, and that she gave each of them a copy of the book *Grandmother's Sunshine.* Jan and I now have those two copies. As far as I know they are the only copies existing.

Generation two. Child or children of Grandmother Aster, name, number and sex unknown, but they must have existed to provide the grandchildren.

Generation three. Callie and Cammie—sisters, probably, or first cousins. Surname or surnames unknown, although it might have been the same as Grandmother Aster's, whatever that was, if they were her son's children. They might have been named Calanda, or Callistamon and Camellia or Camomile because Callie and Cammie appear to be diminutives. Callie is a direct ancestor to Jan, Clarkia and me. Our grandmother, Schizanthus Laurel, just remembered her as an old lady.

Generation four. Callie's child or children. Names unknown. Her sister or cousin Cammie may not have had children since both books came down to Callie's descendants—Little Mum and Aunt Helen had a copy each.

Generation five. Callie's grandchild or grandchildren . . . unknown, but according to Jan, one had the surname Bay.

Generation six. Schizanthus Laurel nee Bay. Married to Bram Laurel. Jan's and my grandmother, whom we called Little Nanna Laurel. Clarkia's great-grandmother.

Generation seven. Schizanthus Laurel's children. Twins. My aunt Hellebore "Helen" Laurel married Lance de Leon. My mother Rose "Rosie" Laurel married Jonathan "Jon" Pearmain.

Generation eight. Aunt Helen's elder daughter—Cousin Lupin de Leon, who was Headmistress of Mary Shelley School for Girls and who then worked for the Vouch-Safe company for a while.

Pip put down her pen. That was all she knew of her past family, and a good deal more than she'd known last week. Magda had been nagging her to find out more. That still seemed odd because she wasn't especially interested in her own patchy genealogy. She claimed it was so she could find out exactly how old Pip's copy of *Grandmother's Sunshine* was. That was just *weird,* but Magda was an agent for actors and artists' models, who also owned a gallery. She said she wanted to know whether the artwork in *Grandmother's Sunshine* was in the public domain.

Much good it would do her if it was, Pip thought. As far as she knew, she and Jan had the only copies of the title, and public domain or not, the physical books were theirs and not Magda's.

Seeing Tamzin Campania drawing a hauntingly familiar copy of one of the illustrations today had shocked Pip to her toenails. For a few seconds she'd thought Tamzin must have a previously unknown third copy. That had turned out to be a false assumption.

After putting together clues and memories, she'd realised Tamzin was the grown-up version of a little girl with whom she had shared stories from the treasured book twenty-five years before. She hadn't made the connection before because Tamzin had once been known as Angie Blake, but once she did work it out the facts came clear. It was Pip's own copy Tamzin remembered and was trying to reproduce for her small daughter.

Pip began to hum in a high, insistent mosquito whine. She often did that when she was contented, and, conversely, when she was uneasy, too. It bothered some people.

Talking to Tamzin about the book they'd both loved for years had brought a sea-change in Pip's mind. She'd been determined to keep her copy in the family, although, admittedly, the name would die out with her and the bloodline with Clarkia . . . unless Clarkia had children.

Seeing Tamzin carefully recreating pictures she'd loved in childhood to share with her daughter, Music, had softened Pip's stance.

She *would* keep her copy of the book and eventually give it to Clarkia, but she saw that maybe Tamzin deserved a copy too. Maybe even Magda did. Magda would display the pictures in her gallery where others could enjoy them. She might sell prints, but why not? Why *shouldn't* people who loved nostalgic illustrations have copies of them to keep? Why *shouldn't* the legacy of Pip's family be spread to strangers' children? They had no children of their own.

To reproduce the book, or even the illustrations, legally, Magda, or someone, would have to be certain the author and illustrator had died more than seventy years ago. Looking at her chart of generations Pip thought this *must* be so.

The book had existed at least since her grandmother Schizanthus Laurel's great-grandmother was a child. It might be much older than that, but Callie, who belonged to generation three, had presumably had the book when she was young. Schizanthus had been born in the 1890s, and Jan said

Schizanthus had *just* remembered Callie as an old lady. Children's notions about age were notoriously unreliable, but even if Callie had been just fifty or so the seventy years must have well-and-truly passed by now.

Pip stopped humming and tapped her pen on the page. Yes. Definitely. Whoever wrote and illustrated *Grandmother's Sunshine* had been gone for well over a century.

That's if they were human . . .

Chapter Two. Cold Tea

Pip threw up her hands in exasperation. It was human copyright law she was trying to appease, so she'd have to assume the author and illustrator were human. If they weren't, then human law was probably immaterial.

She knew some people would disregard copyright law without a qualm. She, Jan and Clarkia, and even Magda couldn't, because they all made their living from the arts in some way. Ignoring copyright would be self-destructive.

Maybe, Grandmother Aster was the person who had made the book and had two copies printed for her grandchildren. That would account for its mythic rarity.

Jonquil Orange, of *The Orange Grove* bookshop, had never seen a copy and thought it was a myth. If it had existed in more than a severely limited edition, and if it had been reprinted and the copyright renewed, then Jonquil would have known.

In any case, Pip was satisfied that more copies could be made, though who they'd belong to, legally and morally, she really didn't know.

It's probably up to Jan and Clarkia and me to decide.

In any case, she'd come as far on the provenance and future of *Grandmother's Sunshine* as she could without consulting the others.

At that point, Pip realised she'd diverged from the topic of *Family* and into the topic of *Book*. She shrugged and decided to call it two topics done in one hit.

A little change to the heading . . . *done.*

She wrote *Further Action* underneath.

Regarding *Grandmother's Sunshine,* talk to Jan and Clarkia about the possibility of creating a new edition, and how far, and whether, it should be restricted.

Regarding the family, no action can be taken because there's nothing I can do.

Even Pip knew it would be terribly intrusive to broach the subject of future children with Clarkia right now, if at all. Her long-term partner had proved duplicitous, and Clarkia was newly single and probably in no mood to consider possible sires for children she might not even want anymore.

Not only that, but she might turn on Pip and demand to know why *she* hadn't put herself out there as a stud mare if she was so invested in the family continuation.

It was never the right time.

Such a lame excuse and barely even true.

I was too self-absorbed.

That was harsh, but probably accurate.

You could adopt.

I could not. I'm probably too old in any case. People might sometimes adopt stray children of their blood, I think, but that comes under the special-circumstances exemption. They might not come right out and say *Too old,* but they'd just quietly put me to the back of the list in favour of people who are younger and who could never have had natural children.

Sighing, Pip turned to a new and happier heading.

Delphine.

The ballet is plotted out, and two pieces of music are secured . . . *Silk and Circumstance* can be used for the entry of the dolphins, and *Porthole Tag,* courtesy of Master Capricorn, for the ship scene.

Jane has arranged for the Forever troupe to workshop the ballet with me, and for Richenda Pendennis to dance the Delphine role. Her fiancé . . . Corin, I think he's called . . . will dance the seafay man.

Actions . . .

Talk to Tamzin and Master Capricorn about the rest of the music. They have both agreed, in principle, to develop the score. I'm talking to Tamzin in the morning after Dance in the Dawn, so that's already arranged. Master Capricorn should be easy to find. I just have to look for the bunch of goats that follow him around or follow the smell of gingerbread. I'm sure he'll help. He said he was available for anyone wanting impromptu music.

Talk to Humph about the recording he made of *Porthole Tag* and get it copied so we can still have it for rehearsals if Master Capricorn is too busy to play live and if Humph is unavailable to play it back.

Talk to the Forever people to find out how much I can and will be involved in the workshopping.

The last line made her feel a bit sad. *Delphine* was the first proper ballet she'd choreographed. She didn't want to relinquish control, but she knew she'd be busy with filming for the rest of the festival. When she was no longer busy with the film, the dance troupe would have returned to their base, or gone on tour or something.

Besides, if a professional company was going to workshop the ballet and possibly perform it, there had to be some trade-off. If she'd stuck to her original idea of putting on the ballet with school children she would have been in charge, and would probably have danced the lead, but it would have been a much simpler and less impressive production.

If—and she was aware it was a *big* if—the Forevers liked the way the ballet developed, they might include it in their future repertoire and that would be—

Pip blinked, feeling a glow of excited wellbeing. That would be—

My legacy to the future!

She beamed. Her Experience was *still* paying dividends.

And it's your legacy too, Lupin! Without you I would never have seen the dolphins and could not have formulated Delphine. *I wish . . .*

Tears pricked the back of her eyes and she blinked furiously before shaking off the feeling and returning to her list. What was done was done and regret would do Lupin no good. In fact, it would be disrespectful to her life and her memory.

Pip didn't know the Forever troupe, but at least she did know Jane Pendennis, and Richenda was Jane's aunt, and Tane's sister, so it should be easy enough to get a meeting with the people who made the decisions.

She gave herself a few seconds to picture a hypothetical Opening Night when she, as originator of the ballet *Delphine,* might properly take a curtain call.

With a huge bouquet.

She would make a deep *reverence* to the troupe who had brought her legacy to life, and she'd say—"This is for you, Lupin!"

And a right berk I'd look, peering through the fronds of a giant bouquet, Pip thought, laughing at herself.

Universe, there is no need for you to make me stub my toe or topple off the stage. I know I'm being vainglorious and ridiculous.

Pip put down the next heading.

Queen of the Clowder and *Caprice.*

Queen is a single scene ballet in which I will dance the old queen cat. Can be done with children after I go home. I need cat music and willing dancers. They need not be proficient, but they do need to be willing and able.

Caprice is a ballet for goats and two goatherds and maybe nymphs and things. Not sure when or even if I can get to that one.

Actions . . . Maybe talk to Master Capricorn—ask for more goat music. He has an affinity with goats.

See if anyone has any ideas for cat music. Ask Tamzin and Matin if time.

Next came the film.

Half-Life of the Lost.

Out of my hands. The main action is to make sure I stay alert and engaged and don't let my mind wander off along byways or down rabbit holes. As Magda said, *Half-Life of the Lost* is the reason I'm here at the festival at all. I have to be on time and stay on track for the sake of my own career, for Magda's, and for the sake of everyone else involved. No mental rambling off and no maundering over chances missed because I'll be hard at work.

Pip flexed her fingers again. With each heading written, explained, and resolved, she felt the buzzing in her brain growing quieter.

She wrote down the next one.

The Fay Puppy Gillan Offered Me.

Gillan St Ives offered to obtain a fay puppy for me so I can experiment with Dog-Morse.

She stopped and considered.

Status—undecided. There are more cons than pros, but most of them boil down to having to make an effort and to put up with having my routine disrupted. It has already been disrupted and may be more so in future if I get more jobs, either through Magda's efforts or from *Half-Life of the Lost* reminding casting people I'm still alive and performing.

Action—First, find out what the cats think of the prospect. Lemonwood Cottage is their home too and they might not want me to import a puppy. They might even leave . . . which would be their prerogative, considering they arrived on their own recognisance and stay by their own choice.

If they are in favour, or neutral, find out if Clarkia would be willing to look after a puppy as well as the cats and the cottage if and when I have to be away.

If the answer is an unequivocal yes, then decide which sort of puppy and ask Gillan to arrange it.

Pip nodded to herself. That seemed sensible, and it allowed

her to put off the decision without feeling she was procrastinating.

What else?

Ah yes. There was more to do on the heading of family.

Make myself more available to Jan and Clarkia if they want to stay in touch. Don't give vague answers or prevaricate if they suggest getting together with me. Be truthful but not tactless in my dealings with them.

She sighed heavily, and added, If they prefer not to be bothered with me, I will accept it with grace. It is my own fault for not bothering with them until it suited me.

In any case, I will make sure I go to Delmsford Flower Show with Jan next February because we have a date with Lupin's ashes and the Clancy Bucket.

Action . . . Just make sure you do it.

Pip flipped the pad shut and clamped the pages with her green pen. She returned it to her messenger bag. She felt strangely light and empty.

She frowned.

There was something else she'd meant to do. What *was* it?

Ah! Pip picked up her cold cup of chamomile tea. She briefly admired the personalised cup before she drank the contents in measured gulps.

Chapter Three. Dancing the Full Hour

After her cathartic hour with her feint-lined pad and her list, Pip went to bed. She didn't wake when Magda came in, but as on the first morning, a bright ruffle of music brought her out of her dreams.

Time to Dance in the Dawn.

She'd always been an early riser, although not necessarily *this* early, and she got out of bed in an anticipatory hurry.

In five minutes she was heading for the circle of lamplight where Tamzin already stood on her dais playing her fiddle.

It was a new tune this morning, and another one Pip didn't know.

Other musicians were joining in. She saw Master Capricorn's rotund figure surrounded as usual by fascinated goats. Mim, seated at her spinet, was beside him. The sound was sharper than a piano and it provided a sparkling backing for the fiddle.

Flutes and the odd drums with added strings joined in. Everyone else seemed to know the piece.

Pip looked at the other dancers. She recognised Jane and her cousin Laura, the lovely Richenda, who was to dance the lead in *Delphine,* Grant Chapman and the rest of Dad Ballet, and Star Calder-Quince, the forty-something actor who was playing the part of Perdita in *Half-Life of the Lost.*

Like Pip herself, Star was no better than competent at ballet, but she had informed Pip that she needed to stay fit because she'd be spending hours of filming time apparently comatose in a hospital bed.

Pip quite liked Star. She was matter-of-fact and down-to-earth without being too blunt or intrusive. She had a pleasantly husky voice, low for a woman, and her smile showed creases in all the right places. If Pip had felt the need for friends, Star would have been a viable candidate.

Don't be silly. You have no idea where she lives, and she's probably got a big family and a mass of lifelong friends vying for her attention already.

Star had presence. She was technically too old to play the bridal version of Perdita, but she had an athletic figure and a timeless face that seemed to be smiling even in repose. That was important. As a comatose protagonist she could use no wiles to enchant an audience, but her finely drawn features and the pleasant curve of her lips would still draw attention and keep her relatable.

She had beautiful hands, too, Pip observed, watching Star dancing, and a nice shape without being runway material. She wore tights under a lemon leotard with a gold bar brooch pinned rakishly to the cleavage. It reminded Pip of something, but she couldn't recall the context.

Then she remembered. *Of course!* Humph had asked Star to wear it visibly so he could identify her.

Not everyone danced the dawn in for the full hour, and Pip saw several dancers arrive or move back into the shadows. Knowing she'd be doing practice with Jane at seven, and spending hours onstage later, she resolved to gear down a bit, but it wasn't easy with that joyous music bubbling and leaping around her.

She eased forwards as she danced, determined to be close to Tamzin Campania when the session wrapped.

Tamzin had agreed to discuss ballet music this morning, but practice was at seven, and who knew when Magda might announce a stage call for the film.

Pip, like Star, was in every remaining scene, so they probably couldn't take advantage of the festival delights during filming as the other cast members would.

To make it even less likely that there would be breaks, the film crew wasn't restricted to the vagaries of light and weather, since all scenes except the prologue, which had been shot on the first day, took place in controlled indoor lighting.

Tamzin paused momentarily, then drew her bow across the strings in a single cry. She played a bright phrase of music and launched into the piece Jane called "Grá Damhsa," which meant *dancing love,* and which was Jane's, and Pip's, favourite.

On the first morning this tune had signified the end of Dancing in the Dawn, so Pip gave up on her efforts at restraint and threw herself into the music. It was more like Irish dancing than ballet, but her feet seemed to know what to do.

The music ceased. Tamzin thanked everyone and invited them to reconvene next morning—unless they'd fancy Dancing Down the Dusk that evening as well.

The dancers, hopped up on endorphins and adrenaline, yelled an enthusiastic assent.

Tamzin exchanged glances with Costas Capricorn, who looked Greek but who Pip had learned was probably a herd-fee man. She pulled a comical face. "Are you up for reconvening at half past five, Master Capricorn?"

The man laughed, shaking the eight-reed pipes above his head. "For you, Mistress Campania, anything."

Tamzin stepped down from her dais, holding out her arms for her daughter, whom her husband, Matin, had brought to watch the last few minutes of the dance.

The tiny girl had brown hair, a shade lighter than her parents', and slightly pointed ears as a legacy of her elf heritage.

Pip wondered if Music Campania should be added to her upcoming list of orders of the fay. Her father was an elf, but

Tamzin was evidently human. The term Magda used for folk like Music was *halfling,* but that might apply to anyone with parents of two different orders as well as to those who were half human.

Jane had said her aunt Richenda was a half-and-half who had *thrown hard* to the pisky blood from her father. Jane herself was an interesting mixture with at least four bloodlines contributing to her DNA.

Pip saw that her list of fay spottings was going to be far more complicated than she'd thought. Maybe she should stick to the fullbloods, but then, how would she know their status unless she asked them? She'd never have guessed Richenda sprang from a fully-human mother. Apart from Tane and Jillian Jules and, okay, the leprechaun men, the blonde dancer was the least ordinary-looking person Pip had ever met.

She glanced over at Star Calder-Quince, who had bent into a half-hoop, grasping her calves, stretching out her muscles after the dance.

Human? Probably. Almost certainly.

But she had *something.*

Presence, Pip supposed. Star was an actor. It was part of the stock-in-trade.

She snapped her attention back to Tamzin and her family. About now it would be lovely to go with Jane to the fossmere, the gorgeous waterfall pool where Jane generally went to swim after ballet practice.

The fossmere was *over there,* where Pip had lately spent a glorious week with Jane's family, and so it was out of her reach to visit it today. Probably. Pip was still learning information regarding the various gateways to *over there,* but she knew that even if there was one close by it wouldn't necessarily debouch anywhere near the fossmere, and in any case she couldn't go through unescorted.

Edgar Treadwell, the big, placid guesthouse keeper in Sydney, had taken her through the gateway in his courtyard into the fay homeland of *over there*, and Ardal Cornfellow, who lived there, had taken her along to the chalklands. When Pip had later tried to go through the gate on her own, just before she and Magda had met Matin Campania to come down to Delphinium Island, she'd ended up in a matching courtyard from the terrace house in the street behind.

She supposed she'd known, intellectually, that it would happen. If it were as easy as walking through a gate, then *over there* would be flooded with accidental tourists. She knew it was pretty well impossible to use the Bass Strait gateway without a fay escort. Even fullbloods found it very difficult unless they had a large helping of water blood.

While inadvertently trespassing in the next garden over, she'd met a fay cat named Rasputin and a gardener called Gabe Angelus who said Rasputin lived with his cousin, Raphael. It had been an interesting encounter, especially with the tom. Before that encounter, Pip had always placed the savage lemon tree and the sly-eyed gooseberry bush in her own garden at Lemonwood Cottage at the head of the queue of her dangerous liaisons. Since then, she'd shuffled Rasputin to the top of the pile. After all, the lemon and the gooseberry could be thwarted by merely staying out of their reach. With the cat, that might prove implausible.

He hadn't threatened her, exactly, but he'd yodelled at her in a bone-chilling wail that displayed his highly effective fangs. She wondered why he chose to live on the human side of the gates. Was he attached to his human landlord, or did he just like lording it over the ordinary cats? Kittisack, one of her own feline housemates, was a fay tom, but he never threatened anyone as far as she knew.

She sighed, longing for the peace and cool water of the fossmere, but there was probably no point in getting cleaned up when she had practice at seven in any case.

She watched Tamzin playing peek-a-boo with her child.

After a couple of minutes, Tamzin gave the baby a kiss and handed her back to Matin. He smiled so lovingly that it made Pip feel peculiar, as if she'd accidently seen something private. Her parents and grandparents had loved one another, but her memories of them dated mostly from the time when they'd been married for years, if not for decades.

Well, if the Campanias wanted to keep that loving bond strictly away from interested onlookers, they should save expressing it for when they were alone, she thought.

"Those two make me feel *sooo* old," Star said in a low voice, laughing.

Pip divined Star was talking to her.

"Do they?" Silly thing to say, as Star had just said they did.

"As a general thing, I *don't* feel old," Star continued.

"You're not," Pip said. She frowned and added, reflectively. "I'm not old, either. "

"Obviously not, since you just danced a full hour."

"Is that how you know when you're old? When you can no longer dance a full hour?"

Star appeared to give that some thought.

Pip began to hum under her breath.

Star looked startled and rubbed the back of her neck before she replied, "I wouldn't say that. I'd say you're old when you no longer *want* to dance the full hour."

"Hm."

"You sound as if you don't agree. That's your prerogative, obviously. Anyone who disagrees with my opinions is *clearly* a moron, but I still defend their right to parade their errors."

Pip ignored that blatant piece of provocation. She broke her humming to say, "I was thinking of the Little Nannas and Pops and Little Mum and Dad. *They* still wanted to – I think. They still *did*, as long as they could."

"Dance, you mean?"

"No. I'm the only one who dances. But *things*. They all had things they loved to do—things that defined them. Little Nanna Pearmain loved to do freeform embroidery, nearly to the end. She was working on the most exquisite scene of ducks in the river when she lost the use of her left side. My dad promised her he'd help her put in the final stitches, and he did. It was done and framed within a couple of weeks, and she was so pleased. He did a lovely job, although of course you can see the difference in their skill. I have it on my wall, and I think of them both when I look at it. My family were all like that—all creative in different ways and they all took a proper interest in one another's projects. Little Dad made matchstick models and donated them for charities to auction. Little Pop Pearmain restored antique furniture and old photographs. They were all naturally talented.

"Little Mum was the last of them. She collected plant catalogues and planned gardens. She could *see* the way things would look. People used to ask for her help and she always gave it. Only—" Pip broke off, feeling a stab of fresh pain. She grimaced and confessed, for the first time, ever, "She filled out an order to a company called *Klein Nederlanden* for some firebird tulip bulbs. She ordered three dozen *random mixed,* and she said she hoped they would have all three shades of red and all three forms represented. There was a fringed form and maybe a classic and a double. She was still missing Dad, I know, but she was still happy and hopeful about those bulbs. I promised to post the order form for her because she was feeling tired."

"And you never did?" Star asked gently.

"I never did. She went to glory the same day. It seemed—" Pip turned out her hands.

"Maybe you're not a tulip person."

"I'm not, really. I'm more of a daisy person. Or marigolds. I *like* marigolds, especially the calendula type. But I said I'd do it. It was practically a promise. So I should have posted the order and planted the bulbs in Little Mum's garden."

"Maybe you still can."

"I don't live there anymore."

Star gave her a sudden grin. "*That* needn't stop you. Tell you what, you order the bulbs, and when they come, call and let me know. You and I will make an expedition. We'll take those firebirds to your mum's old garden and plant them in the dead of night, then do a dance of homage dedicated to her. Deal?" She held out her hand.

Pip hesitated. "I live in Tasmania, you know."

"I didn't know, but so what? Lovely part of the world. Let's make a pact. It's a daft thing to do, but everyone should be daft once in a while. It's good for the soul."

Pip was fairly certain she was daft *all* the time, but she laid her hand in Star's.

"Brilliant!" Star said. She danced five tiptoe steps. "If the cops catch us, what would be the charge do you think?"

"Not theft," Pip said.

"No . . . adding tulips without the owner's consent? Entering a garden with intent to plant? Trespass with bulbs in a bucket?"

"Could be, but not *criminal* trespass. It's not as if I was going there to dig up someone's buried treasure or make away with knickers off a clothesline."

"That's called snowdropping. Sounds so innocent . . ."

"Gathering flowers by the wayside," Pip agreed.

Star nodded vigorously and bent to pluck an imaginary flower. "So they'd let us off with a caution at the most," she said, admiring it. "We're ladies of a *certain age* and we can look baffled and flustered and apologetic on cue. It's a date, then. Your Little Mum will be cheering us on. *My* mum certainly will be if I tell her the tale."

"Will you tell her?"

"Wouldn't you have told yours? If you did something

dodgy but harmless?"

"I don't know. Mum was *good,* you see. Transparent and kind. She thought I was better than I was. Better than I am, I mean."

"I doubt if she really did. It's a mum's job to love well, but to see clearly. I'm sure she knew you and loved you just as you were. Her creation set free." She laughed, suddenly. "My mum's name is Clearsky, can you believe it? In one word. Think of growing up with *that* when all your friends are called Susan, Wendy, Vicki, and Jennifer."

"I like it, but you're right—it's unusual. Mind, you, there can't be too many people called Star, either," Pip pointed out.

"No. When I ventured to complain about *not* being called Renae, or Kelly or Christy like my friends, Mum would always say if she could survive Clearsky, even when it was raining, Star was a walk in the park—even in daylight. If she'd ever managed another baby, she was going to call it Saturday. Imagine. Saturday Fortunato." Star shook her head and slid back into her plan without a pause. "Once they're planted, we can go back at the relevant time and see if they're flowering." Star pushed back her hair. "Ick. I need a shower. Give me your contacts later, so we can arrange the date for our horticultural misdemeanour."

She gave Pip a final grin, blew an airy kiss, and danced away.

Chapter Four. Breakfast Al Fresco

"Are you two plotting to commit grand larceny?" Tamzin sounded interested and not a bit censorious.

Pip turned to face her. "The opposite of larceny, though you might call it a grand enterprise. Do you remember the garden where we used to pick flowers when you were little?"

"I think so . . . was there a lilypond? With a wooden bridge?"

"Yes. And goldfish."

"I remember! They were enormous and they had white blotches! And there was an old cat that used to watch the fish and stick his front paw in the pond, and then shake it. He belonged to an old lady with white hair . . .oh! That must have been your mum. Maybe I do remember her after all. I have a mind picture of her kneeling beside the cat and wearing gloves with flowers on them, and a floppy green hat. She was tiny, like you. She used to call me Butterfly."

"So she did! I'd forgotten. The cat was called Duster. Right. You *do* remember. Well, Star and I were planning to go back there to my mother's garden and plant tulips in her memory."

"Not larceny then."

Pip shook her head. She didn't feel the need to explain that she no longer lived in the family home and thus might be said to have forfeited her right to plant tulips there. "Have you time to discuss dance music now?" she ventured.

"That was the arrangement." Tamzin raised fine brows. "Come and have a cup of tea and some breakfast al fresco. Walk me through your ballet, so I can get an idea of the style of music that's wanted."

Pip went willingly with Tamzin to an outdoor café where the fair-haired waiter was taking orders for breakfasts.

They settled at a table and Tamzin smiled widely at the waiter. "Hey, Dequan. Can we have whatever's best? Oh, and tea for me and—" She glanced at Pip.

"Cambric tea," Pip said hopefully. He'd given her some the day before.

He nodded and turned back to Tamzin. "Want chips with that, *schat*?"

Tamzin laughed and shook her head.

"*Chips*?" Pip asked when he had gone. "*Schat*?"

"In-joke." Tamzin gazed after the waiter, still smiling. "I was in love with him for *so* long. Ten years or so."

"Not now?"

"That would hardly be appropriate. I'm married to someone else. And no, truly, not now. I still do love him. I always will, I expect, but I love Matin so much *more.* Dequan is incidental music. Matin is the full symphony. Still—Dequan and I know a disturbing amount about one another. The significance of chips, for instance. And *schat* is a kind of pet-name he picked up from his mother. She was born in the Netherlands, and though she came out as a child, she's bilingual."

"Is *he* married?" Pip asked. She wondered but managed not to ask if the smiling waiter was still carrying a torch . . . and chips . . . for Tamzin. That would be awkward. Pip didn't *do* awkward.

"He is! He found a wonderful woman called Martina to love." Tamzin smiled fondly. "They have in-jokes referencing geese and feathers and egg-bread and shirts that I don't understand. Matin and I have in-jokes about shoes and apples, frozen peas and eavesdroppers that Dequan and Martina don't understand. I can't tell you how *happy* that makes me feel. Matin's and my frozen peas make Dequan's and my chips look like a mere shadow in comparison."

She turned her attention to Pip. "Right. Ballet. And—" She waved vigorously and beckoned to someone approaching from behind Pip's chair. "Master Capricorn! Please detach those goats and come over here! We're talking about ballet music, and we need your input."

The friendly herdfee strolled up. There was a pause while he handed out sticky gingerbread to six goats. Four of them took the treat and trotted off, but two lingered, chewing, making their beards jerk sideways.

"*Antio, sas,*" Capricorn said, making a shooing motion.

The two, a milk-white nanny and a rakish-looking billy with black stockings, gave him identical calculating looks, bleated defiantly, and retreated.

Tamzin laughed. "Nanny Lutana always has to have the last word."

"What's the billy's name?" Pip asked.

Capricorn sat down opposite her. "Who knows? He's her current favourite paramour. *I* call him Uncle Evilbeard because he doesn't care to tell me his real name. He hasn't objected."

Goat-Morse? And what a perfect name!

Tamzin looked expectantly at Pip.

Pip saw she was waiting to talk music and ballet and pulled her thoughts away from perfectly-named goats.

"A ballet?" Capricorn prompted.

Pip nodded. "*Delphine* tells the story of a woman who knows the dolphins," she said. "The ballet starts with the dolphins swimming into the scene—that's *Silk and Circumstance.* They dive to a shipwreck and swim in and out—and that music is "Porthole Tag"." She tilted her chin at the herdfee. "That's the tune you invented for us."

"On the amphora horn," he said.

"That's it. After that tune, one of them—a minor soloist—finds some treasure, and it swims away and fetches Delphine, the first principal. She swims down to see what they have found, and they dance. A seafay man enters, and the dolphins scatter."

"They're afraid of him?" Costas Capricorn asked.

"Yes."

"Why?"

"Why?" Pip scowled. It seemed self-evident to her.

Tamzin laughed suddenly. "Come on, Master Capricorn . . . you know our good friend Mariner. Anyone would be scared of him!"

"You *know* a seafay man?" Pip asked. "Socially?" It seemed so unlikely—like taking tea with a Bengal tiger.

Tamzin nodded vigorously. "In the manner of speaking, although we don't exactly go to the movies together. He's our most alarming acquaintance . . . other than his wife Meribelle. Now she's seriously scary. My husband is *terrified* of her, and so is Mariner. She tries to drown him on a regular basis. It will never do him any harm, obviously, but the pride in him that she tries so hard is overweening!"

"He wants her to drown him?"

"No, but he wants her to try. It's proof of her continued interest in him, apparently. If she were a complaisant wife he'd feel he'd failed. I think. That's my understanding of it—I've never actually asked them."

"That sounds accurate enough to me. There must be pursuit. *Quite* unlike the way my folk manage things." Capricorn turned to Pip. "I take it you know someone from the seafay order too?"

"I don't know any personally, but I did see one when I was *over there* with Tane Pendennis."

Tamzin looked as if she was planning to ask questions about that, but Capricorn got in first. "You're not referring to the impressive Master van der Strand, I take it?"

"No—Tane said the one I saw was called Lore Mor

Arlodh." She brought the complex name out with care. "Tane told me how to greet him politely if we did meet face to face, but as it happened, we didn't. His wife is called Mistress Xanthe. Apparently if we had met up he would have insulted me, but I would then have been at liberty to insult him back. Except that Xanthe might have got in first." She shook her head, still perplexed. "It sounds unbelievable, saying it out loud, but Tane made it seem logical. It seems to match up with what you said about the ones you know."

"Don't know the couple you mentioned, but they sound typical," Capricorn said thoughtfully. He added, "Xanthe isn't a seafolk name, however."

"I don't think she is seafolk, unless the women look different to the men, the way the leprechauns do. She wasn't—um—greenish or scary, but I saw her dive off the cliffs." Pip started to hum. It had never occurred to her to wonder why dolphins would be afraid of a seafay man . . . other than the obvious *scariness* of a man with silver green skin and fearsome demeanour and, according to Tane, a fine collection of insults.

When she'd first thought of her ballet she'd meant the tension to come from a shark or a giant squid, but then she'd decided the seafay man would be a better fit, dramatically speaking.

She broke off her humming to ask, "Do seafay eat dolphins?"

Tamzin said, "I wouldn't think so. No. I'm sure Mariner and Meri don't. We've seen them leaping out in the charms, and neither of them mentioned wanting to catch them. And they would have. They eat fish and sea vegetables . . . with olives. They like figs and grapes, too, and samphire . . . oh, and tomatoes, although they don't grow them. It's a kind of Mediterranean diet. They don't cook much, if at all. I'm pretty sure they dry their fish rather than smoke them."

"They're territorial though," Capricorn said.

"Glory, yes! Even though they regard Matin and me as friends we formally ask for safe passage when we take the sailing dinghy through their area. Now and again Mariner wants to play forfeits before he gives us a pass." Tamzin grinned, shaking her head as if amused by a thought. "His forfeits are always rather original, and they never fail to annoy Meri."

"What if the seafay man had treasure in the sunken ship?" Pip ventured, reverting to the main subject of conversation.

"And that's what the dolphins found you mean? I think that would work. Mariner has all sorts of odd things in his lair, and you may be sure Matin and I would never touch them without direct invitation. He finds the most extraordinary items, because of course he has sea-gift, and he can prowl on the seabed for far longer than anyone else I know. He has a kelpie bottle, and a tiny ship carved out of coral. He has a collection of shells I've never seen anywhere else. Even Matin hasn't." She glanced at Pip as if wondering if she had to define the sea-gift term, but Pip understood because Tane and his mother Mama Tam had shared something similar with her during her holiday Experience *over there.* Their form of sea-gift, or water gift, had involved giving her what she thought of as super-oxygenated air which allowed her to stay under water for a few minutes rather than for a few seconds. She assumed the seafay man Tamzin knew used it for himself.

Tamzin continued, "Meribelle wears a belt of those beautiful shells, and just lately she's started wearing a coral and pearl bracelet. I think it's a kind of baby present from Mariner because they have a little lad around the same age as our daughter."

Pip didn't much want to dwell on thoughts of special celebratory jewellery, but she relaxed. "That's why the dolphins scatter, then. They found the seafay's treasures and he takes exception to their messing with it."

"You'll want some ferocious music for that part," Capricorn said. "Kettledrums? And horns?" He tapped out a rhythm on the tabletop with two spoons.

"And maybe a much faster and slightly discordant version of *Silk and Circumstance* for the fleeing dolphins," Tamzin suggested. "Would that work, Pip?"

"Do you have music for the kettledrums?" Pip asked, watching the flying spoons. She was sure Costas Capricorn was a good bit older than she was, but his hands were equally as free from signs of arthritis as hers. She wondered if he, too, relied on strawberries and cream to keep his joints in order, or possibly goat cheese and olives. He certainly *looked* as if he enjoyed his food.

Tamzin said, "Master Capricorn will want to see the steps danced—he creates music on the spot, unlike me. I just interpret it."

There was nothing *just* about Tamzin's fiddle-playing, but Pip supposed she had a point.

Capricorn's spoons galloped to a crescendo before he suddenly put them down, apologising to the waiter who was standing patiently with a tray.

Pip watched while tea was dispensed, along with a powerfully-scented coffee for the herdfee. A plate of fruit bread and various bowls of condiments accompanied it and Pip put a piece in her mouth before getting up and sketching the seaman's entrance.

"I don't have the strength or the precision to do this justice," she said.

"Just a walkthrough gives enough of an idea," Tamzin said cheerfully.

Pip finished, then said, "Delphine rushes in to intercept the seafay then and beguiles him while the dolphins escape. Then comes the major *pas de deux* . . ."

Capricorn was nodding attentively. "You might want a

different set of instruments for the dry-land scenes, and a theme for Delphine." He picked up the spoons again.

Pip said to Tamzin, "How do I get permissions to use this music?"

Tamzin said, "If you use any of my existing recordings I'll expect an acknowledgment. If it's put together in a full soundtrack, we'll have a royalty-sharing agreement for the sales."

"I don't own the rights to any of the music."

"No, but the concept and compilation is yours. This will be a tuneful ballet with a lot of dramatic changes, so there might be a demand for the score." She raised crossed fingers. "I'm hoping so. I feel so."

"Don't look at me, mistress," Capricorn said, grinning, "I just play it to the universe. I don't write it down."

"We'll have to grab Humph then, for a start, and later on Matin can lay down proper tracks in the studio if you will oblige. It *will* have to be written down or transcribed, because it might need to be done with live music in many different venues. Do the dolphins return after the seafay drives them off, Pip?"

Pip nodded. "Originally, I meant to do a transformation scene where they changed into cats, but I dropped that."

"Pity," Tamzin said. "Cats are beautiful beings."

"It's not going to waste. I made the concept into a separate single scene ballet which will be much less ambitious.

"For *Delphine,* the dolphins will need to return, but I thought that could be worked into a curtain call where the seafay and Delphine come to take their bows and dance a short ensemble with the pod."

Capricorn put down the spoons and made wavy hand motions.

"Oh, and I forgot the fiddler crabs," Pip continued. "The Dads will do that as a kind of corps de ballet, all knees and elbows. We'll need some syncopated fiddle music for that . . .

if there is such a thing."

The herdfee's hands jerked in a sharp rhythm. "Pizzicato," he said.

Tamzin said, "Maybe one tune at a time, Master Capricorn?"

The herdfee laughed. "That's no fun!" He seized a chunk of fruit bread, covered it with soft cheese and crammed it into his mouth. He swilled it down with coffee so powerful it reminded Pip of the horrid brew Zach's girlfriend had made for him on *Tulpenmanie* at the beginning of Pip's Vouch-Safe Experience.

It seemed so long ago, but it really wasn't. Less than two weeks ago, in fact.

"Is there singing?" he asked.

"What?"

Tamzin said, gently, "I think ballet is all expressed in dance, Master Capricorn."

The herdfee sighed. "I heard a chorus building to a crescendo—" He moved his hands as if conducting a choir. "Right up there—then!" He snapped his fingers. "Everyone stops. Music stops. Dancers freeze. Curtain."

Pip felt her eyes widening. That absolutely didn't happen in ballet, but it would be *splendid.* If the seafay held Delphine in an overhead lift . . .

"How about—" Capricorn broke off suddenly, staring behind Pip.

Pip turned slowly and beheld Magda Saxer, wrapped in her embroidered shawl and tapping her foot as if she'd been waiting for some time to be acknowledged.

"Yes?" Pip said.

"You're onstage in just over an hour," Magda said.

Pip uttered a squeak. "Is it seven already?"

"Ten past," Magda said.

Pip got up, gabbled thanks and an apology to Tamzin and

Capricorn, and fled.

Jane was already well into her exercises, with her cousin Laura and Star Calder-Quince dancing alongside.

Pip joined in, noting that the male half of the dark young couple from the Forever troupe was playing the flute for them. His partner was dancing an energetic *pas de deux* with the enormous braeman she'd seen the day before. She'd deduced he was one of the three people who ran the troupe. The couple matched poorly in size, but they were clearly having fun.

Jane switched to her left leg and spotted Pip. "There you are, Miss Pippin! Are you coming to the rehearsal this afternoon?"

"Rehearsal?" Pip did a set of demi plies to loosen her knees.

"Yes, Hamish said Gervie wanted to see the blocking so far."

Hamish. That was the kilted giant dancing just a few steps away. For such a substantial man, he was light on his feet. Gervie? No clue.

Pip opened her mouth to say of *course* she'd be there, but then she remembered the filming. She *wanted* to be at the ballet rehearsal. She was *obligated* to be at the filming. "I will be there if I can," she hedged.

Jane seemed happy with that—happier than Pip was, anyhow.

When they finished their practice, Pip felt her brain buzzing with events and ideas.

She desperately wanted to retire to cabin six and sit in solitude for an hour or so with her bucket list, but she knew there wouldn't be time.

She closed her eyes for a few seconds. Sorting chaos last night had helped but now it was all crowding in on her again.

Someone touched her arm. Pip jumped. "Yes?"

Star was looking down at her with sympathy. "We're not

old, but we do need to pace ourselves," she said.

Pip said, tersely, "I should think I'm at least twenty years older than you, and probably rather more. You don't look more than forty—if that."

"Yes, I *am* younger, and I get to lie down and zone out with Caraway's Comforts while you're going to be improvising and thinking on your feet in every scene. I couldn't begin to do what you have to do as Solace. It must be *so* hard."

It wasn't *hard,* but Pip had long given up trying to explain that performing was just something she did instinctively . . . a weird talent for which she got paid. "I'll go to bed earlier tonight," she said, as if that were an answer.

"Oh, so shall I . . . and I'm going to take an hour of the lunch time to find somewhere quiet to put my mind back in order."

Pip took that comment to be an oblique suggestion to do the same. She wasn't much of a one for advice, but she thought that this time, she might take it. After all, she'd begun with her therapeutic list-making the evening before.

Chapter Five. Mother

Filming continued throughout much of the day. Pip kept her skittering mind on the job and was pleasantly surprised by how much was done by the end.

It probably helped that they were using a single set, although it was redressed at intervals to show the passing of time. Some of the set-dressing was done by the actors, in character. Medical staff occasionally manhandled updated equipment into position, and old visitors' chairs were exchanged for new ones. A digital clock appeared—Perdita's bedcover was swapped for new ones, becoming first more personal then less so as the years ticked by.

In one scene, Perdita's mother came in with her knitting. She sat casting on stitches for a sweater while she talked to her oblivious daughter.

In Mother's next scene, the garment was almost done. Later still, she came in wearing the sweater because, as she said to the silent figure in the bed, *you don't need it in here, my love . . . I'll make you another one for when you wake. It's a better option than packing this one away in lavender.*

"Or mothballs," Pip, in her role as Solace ad-libbed. She moved over behind Mother and sniffed the air. "You've been making your special lasagne again." She twirled to look at the glucose mixture being drip-fed into Perdita's tube, and quipped, "Never thought we'd be on a liquid diet ever again after all that thin cabbage soup we drank to fit into that wedding dress. Should have eaten the lasagne, the way you advised. I'm sorry, Mum." She embraced the figure in the chair, who took no notice.

Because of the time progression in the set, the scenes were filmed in chronological order. That made it much easier for Pip to manage her ad libs and improvisations. Mother's final scene, however, was shot out of order, because the Mother actor had somewhere else she needed to be. Paradoxically, perhaps, she was going to her real-life daughter's wedding.

When Mother entered, an hour after her previous scene was shot, Pip scarcely recognised her. Someone – possibly the director, or maybe even Humph, had decided not to use heavy latex to age the characters, but to allow posture and clothing to do its job. Mother shuffled in, wearing down-at-heel slippers, shapeless pants and the sweater, which was supposably thirty years older, now faded and unravelling at the collar.

Mother slumped in the armchair next to the bed for a while, telling Perdita news of her week, referencing a scatter of events to date the scene to the early 1990s. Her conversation wandered.

After a bit she mentioned the heat, and the stuffiness of the room.

She took off the sweater to reveal a dull-coloured, mis-buttoned blouse, very different from the neat pastel clothing she'd worn in earlier scenes.

Mother was supposed to sit awhile, as the light faded to black, but Pip, seeing the sweater sliding off her lap in an unscripted movement, hurried to the chair.

"I'll take this now, Mum. I know you made it for me."

Mother, not expecting a Solace cue right there, glanced up. Pip slowly put on the sweater, rolling up the sleeves, and turning as if before a mirror.

"There, do you like it? Thank you!" She kissed Mother on the forehead.

Mother smiled up at her and spoke off-script, proving Pip

wasn't the only one who could improvise. "Darling—you look so lovely!"

"And . . . *cut*!"

Pip waited for censure, but apparently all was well.

Mother got up from the chair, shed forty years, and looked down towards the cameras and director. "Okay with that, camera one?"

Steward stuck his thumb up.

"I'll be here until tomorrow at three, if you need retakes, and I'll make myself available as soon as I'm back from the wedding," Mother said. She was on her way out and on the phone to her daughter before anyone could answer.

Chapter Six. Rehearsal with Dolphins

The break for lunch was short, and they worked solidly in the afternoon.

Jasper Diamond professed himself pleased with their progress and released them at half past three.

Pip saw Star Calder-Quince wiping off her pale makeup as she headed away from the sound stage, presumably taking her own advice regarding having some quiet time away from the bustle to unwind.

Pip would have liked to do the same, but her ballet was calling, so she slipped out of her costume and into her festival dress. It was the green one with butterflies on it, and the patch proclaiming her to be a star. She'd been a bit annoyed by that patch initially, but now she, and everyone else, just accepted it. She'd grown fond of the dress, which moved when she did, fitting loosely without falling off her shoulders or bunching around the waist. Besides, the patch was buttoned on, and knowing she could remove it if and when she chose made all the difference.

Magda was talking to Ward about the embroidered shawl she habitually wore, which seemed to fascinate him, turning it over to show the design on both sides. Pip raised a hand in farewell, walked out into the afternoon, and looked around, getting her bearings.

Where to?

The Icehouse pavilion where she'd obtained her dress and

her festival shirt was still doing its trade in jewellery, clothing, musical instruments, and all kinds of craft.

Someone was demonstrating how to make moulded felt shoes, and someone else was holding a small class in Irish dance. Pip's feet stuttered as she half-recognised the teacher, a young woman with piled up red hair and an elaborate blue costume.

Who . . . Oh! She almost laughed at herself. Of course, it was Liffey Rosheen, who was married to one of Tane's half-brothers—Jane's uncle Finn Rivers. She'd met Liffey during her Experience at the fossmere, but she hadn't expected to find her here at the festival. Tane hadn't mentioned she was coming, but then—he wouldn't necessarily know.

That's one more for my *orders of the fay* list, Pip thought smugly. Then she recalled she hadn't started writing it. She knew Liffey was a leprechaun colleen, but she didn't understand a lot regarding them, having not yet read the fourth *Orders of the Fay* volume concerning *Leprechauns, Piskies and Pixies*. She was still absorbing the mysteries of Volume Two in between working and finding her feet at the festival. At this rate, she wouldn't be finished with the books before it was time to return them to their owners at the guesthouse.

Never mind, she had her own set coming from *The Orange Grove*. With luck, it would be waiting for her when she got home to Lemonwood Cottage.

Irish dancing looked like fun, she thought, watching Liffey demonstrating the correct arm position—apparently one didn't lift the arms the way one did for Scottish dance—but she had a ballet rehearsal to track down.

She walked on, scanning left and right, hoping to see someone she might ask. Unfortunately, most of those who knew where to go would be there already.

Another group of dancers made her pause, but the elaborate dress the female presenter had on looked all wrong for ballet. She was small and dark, wearing high heels and a gold fish-tailed gown, whirling in the arms of a fair-haired man with blue eyes.

She paused, gesturing to the rest of the group to join in. Pip had done a bit of ballroom dancing in the film *Hitchhike Hilaria,* but she hadn't kept it up. Unlike ballet, it wasn't something one could easily practise alone.

The men of Dad Ballet were dancing a respectful distance away, some of them dressed in their signature *dad* clothing of khaki work shorts worn with blue singlets and boots, and the others in workout gear with towels around their necks.

Evidently they were presenters, because their singlets sported their names and *Dad Ballet* and they had twenty or so assorted men in mufti working through basic ballet exercises.

Grant Chapman, who had danced with Pip's group the day before and again this morning, flicked her a thumbs up gesture. She had no idea why.

She was so busy pondering that she ran straight into Jane Pendennis. The girl looked startled for a second before her face lit into its beatific smile. "Miss Pippin! You're coming to the rehearsal after all! I'm so *glad.*"

"So will I be, if I can find it," Pip said, stepping back. Jane was excitable and affectionate, and quite likely to fling her arms around her.

"This way!" Jane beckoned her towards one of the onsite buildings. Pip was unsure what to call it. It *looked* like a large hall lit with skylights and huge windows, but it had a temporary air, as if it might be taken down at any moment. It wasn't as big as the Icehouse, but Pip thought it looked bigger than the barn where she'd met Tamzin and finally recognised her as the one-time Angie Blake.

Jane led her inside, where she beheld Tamzin with her fiddle and Costas Capricorn surrounded by a variety of instruments, some familiar and some not. Mim the spinet player was there, quietly running through some notes with the young dark-haired couple. The boy had his flute and the girl held something that looked like a tambourine with an extra metal ring.

Several members of the Forever troupe were walking through steps that Pip recognised, after a confused moment, as the treasure-finding part of the ballet.

A tall fair man seemed to be overseeing them. He looked hauntingly familiar.

Not Dequan, the tall, fair waiter.

Pip caught Jane by the arm. "Who's that?"

Jane said, "That's Master Almaclair."

"I thought the great big braeman who was dancing with the dark girl this morning was Master Almaclair."

"He's Master Hamish Almaclair. This one is Master Gervais."

Pip set aside the fact that the men didn't look like brothers. She said, "Is this one any relation to Court Leopold?"

"The *Courtesan* lutist? I don't think so. Why?"

"They look so much alike, only this one is a lot older. I thought maybe he was his father or uncle."

Jane looked thoughtfully at the elegant fair-haired man and shook her head. "How do you mean, alike?"

Pip thought that was obvious. "Hair, eyes, the way they stand, the way they—" She flipped her hand, unable to put it into words. Then it came to her. "The air of *superior courtesy.* Sir Galahad crossed with Paul Messenger—that guy from the comic."

Jane's expression brightened. "I don't know what comic you mean, but I see what you're saying! You might be picking up a likeness because Master Almaclair and Master Leopold are both courtfolk men from pureblood families."

Pip knew enough to understand the term *pureblood* didn't have any connotations of class among the fay. It simply denoted that someone was of a single bloodline rather than mixed. Jane herself was an interesting mixture, but no one would ever think the less of her because of it.

Pip thought back to the first volume of *The Orders of the Fay* which she'd read with close attention while still at the Treadwells' guesthouse. *Alpenfee, Braefolk and Courtfolk.* Of course!

She said, "That's right. I read about that. They all marry people from their own order, so they tend to reinforce the genes. That means they look alike."

"*Mostly,* they do," Jane corrected. "In theory. Master Leopold's lady isn't courtfolk though, and Mistress Flori Almaclair is human, like you. And—" She glanced at the cluster of musicians. "You see Amalie over there?" She indicated the dark girl with the tambourine. "She's pure court, but Tim—her man there—is a court quarterling."

"What's the rest?" Pip asked.

Jane considered the young man. "Pixie and human. He and his brothers are friends with Sam—my big sister from Jules." She added, "Come and see what's been done so far."

Pip glanced from the musicians to the dancers and back. She had no idea how to join the group without seeming silly or presumptuous or both.

Jane solved the problem by taking her hand and towing her over to where the dolphins were excitedly clustering.

Gervais Almaclair glanced over his shoulder. "Amalie!"

The dark tambourine girl darted across and joined the huddle of dolphins.

"Amalie's the dolphin soloist," Jane whispered.

The spinet and amphora horn joined in with a tune that was *almost Silk and Circumstance,* but not quite, and the soloist danced a short passage in which she informed her pod, in expressive mime, that she would fetch their friend to see what they'd found. She held the tambourine aloft and danced away.

The steps weren't exactly what Pip had laid down, and for a few seconds she felt the pang of loss for the original simple ballet, but Jane was getting the dancing master's attention.

"Master Gervie, *here*'s Miss Pippin at last!"

He turned and smiled at Pip with considerable charm, holding out his left hand.

He smelled of rosewater, which was delightful but odd.

Pip hesitated. "You're lefthanded like Jan," she said.

His brows went up. "Is that a problem?"

Pip shook her head sheepishly. "I just wasn't sure which I—" She held out her hands. "My cousin is lefthanded, but I don't shake hands with *her*."

"Why would you?" Almaclair took her left one and shook it gravely. "I'm glad you could make it, Miss—" He paused, and added, "What do you prefer to be called?"

"Pip will do."

"Then you'd better call me Gervais. Or Gervie. We've been at this for half an hour because your agent couldn't tell us what time you'd be available. Would you like to see it from the beginning, or shall we push on with the entry of Delphine?"

"From the beginning?" Pip said hopefully.

"Good choice. We'll have a straight run through." He clapped his hands. "From the top! Short overture on the note!"

Pip hadn't considered an overture. She felt sheepish and amateur, but there was no point in sulking. An overture was in place.

She looked over to the musicians. Capricorn gave her a cheerful nod and raised the amphora horn to his lips.

A vibrating note came from somewhere stage left and Capricorn blew into the horn.

Its haunting tone made a shiver run down Pip's spine. A light patter of drumbeats rose behind the horn along with soft notes from the spinet.

A handsome dark-eyed young man raised a strange flute that looked as if it was carved from driftwood. He wore a clerical collar, which seemed odd, but then—why not?

The music swelled until Pip almost thought she heard the beat of waves. A second flute and Tamzin's magical fiddle joined in and played a bright tune before dying away, leaving just the amphora horn and the driftwood flute playing softly until they moved into the familiar waltz.

Someone must have been conducting, but Pip had her focus on the dancers, who in turn were watching Gervie Almaclair.

He nodded to them and called, "Dolphins enter on three . . . one, two, three!"

He stepped back next to Pip as a dozen dancers, a mix of young men and women, moved into the first scene. The dark girl, Amalie, was with them, and so was her young partner, who was dancing and playing his flute at the same time.

Pip watched, entranced. The troupe had dressed in a selection of tights, leotards, shorts and festival shirts, but they moved in beautiful precision.

A horn sounded above the music and Amalie *discovered* the sunken ship.

The music shifted to the tune Pip thought of as *Porthole Tag* as the dolphins played and explored, leaping and darting.

They found the treasure and Amalie—must give her a name for the program, Pip thought—moved into her solo before dancing offstage and returning, almost immediately, with the blonde dancer Jane called Richenda.

She argued in mime with Amalie, explaining through gesture that she couldn't submerge to the depth of the ship.

Pip had never worked out how to handle this part, but evidently Forever had, because Amalie slipped off one of her bracelets and handed it to Richenda.

Pip almost laughed, because Richenda was a pisky halfling and already wore more silver adornments than most humans would ever adopt in a lifetime. Nevertheless, she accepted it, and followed Amalie, first with caution, then with confidence, down to the ship, where she admired the treasure, and danced her first solo, joined by the dolphins.

Pip waited excitedly for the seafay's entrance, but the music sighed to a close, and the dancers fell out of formation and moved forward to surround Almaclair and Pip.

The musicians crowded in too, and for a few seconds Pip was afraid of being squashed.

Jane took her arm and hugged it. "Wasn't it *wonderful*?"

Pip became slowly aware that everyone was looking at her. She swallowed. "It was—was—"

"Somewhat rough, I know," Almaclair said. He regarded his troupe. "But on the whole, not bad at all." He fastened his gaze on Richenda. "Richie you know—you *do* know—you will have to leave off your silver, right?"

The blonde looked annoyed.

"You *will*. Not only will any audience wonder why a single bracelet can give you sea-gift when you're already rattling like a pub till on Friday night, but they'll also wonder how you expect to swim in it."

"I know, oh, master," she said. She dropped him a grand *reverence* then fastened her attention on Pip. "Do you approve?"

Pip nodded. She had a lump in her throat that almost prevented her from speaking.

Jane went on hugging Pip's arm, and she was vaguely grateful for the support.

"It looks good to me." That was scarcely effusive, but it was all she could manage.

Tamzin came up and detached her from Jane. "Is the music we're working up close to what you thought of?"

"No. It's far beyond what I expected. I thought we could use public domain existing tunes, but these are perfect. All those marvellous instruments! I don't know what half of them are."

Tamzin laughed. "You can blame our friend Costas for that. I believe he's quite taken with the idea of having some of his music preserved—especially since he doesn't have to do the preserving."

"That's my job!" Pip heard the voice but had to look for the speaker.

Finally she realised it was Humph, rocking cheerfully on his toes and holding his black recording gadget aloft as if it was a trophy.

"I'll have this transcribed in a day or so," he said.

"That long, eh?" someone called from the crowd.

"Do I know you?"

"No."

"Then I'd better explain that I'm making a film too . . ." His voice trailed away as he perceived Pip. "Um, hello?"

"Hello," Pip said.

Humph frowned. "I know *you*, don't I?"

"I'm in your film."

"So you are!" He fished his tuning fork out of his pocket. "Do you think this might come in handy onstage? At the opening of the next scene . . . it's either that or bells tolling in the distance as Mother dies offscreen."

"You should probably talk to the director," Pip said.

"I will. Yes." Humph nodded. "You're *not* my cousin . . . are you? Um . . . Too small." He gave her a genial nod and turned to Almaclair. "I'll send the transcript to you when it's done. Give me a call when you need me for the next act. Have you got my number?"

"I don't believe so." Almaclair produced a pen from somewhere and handed it over.

Humph scribbled down his number on a piece of card and handed it back.

Then he went out.

There was a disconcerted silence.

Tamzin said, cautiously, "Was that a wee bit—odd?"

Nobody answered.

Pip wondered if she should explain Humph's condition as Star had explained it to her, but she couldn't remember the word for it, let alone spell it, so she held her peace.

Chapter Seven. Rainbow Shoes

To Pip's surprise and pleasure, Almaclair, Tamzin, and Capricorn, who seemed in charge as much as anyone was, consulted her regarding a plan for the next day's rehearsals.

"We thought that since you're involved with the filming over at the soundstage, we might do the first rehearsal in the morning before the auditions and do a straight run-through on the second act in the late afternoon when you can be available," Gervie said.

"Auditions?" Jane said quickly.

Richenda came over and took her aside, putting an affectionate arm around the younger girl. Pip remembered she was Jane's aunt, although she seemed just a few years older. She looked around twenty, and Jane had said she was betrothed.

That was the same as engaged, Pip supposed.

"That would work well for me," Pip said. "Though I can't guarantee we'll be finished filming on time every day. It's not my call."

"Obviously. It seems your . . . what is he exactly?" Gervie, who was tall, held his hand expressively at chest height.

"You mean Humph?"

"If he's the man with the quiff and the recording device who just gave me his number."

"He's Humphrey Carpenter-Rivers, the person who wrote the script of the film I'm in," Pip said. She also thought of Humph as tuning fork man, since he'd been wielding one when she first clapped eyes on him. He was an oddity, but she was inclined to cut him some slack. He loved his work, and besides, he was small, which put her in mind of her beloved Little Pops Pearmain and Laurel and Little Dad. Unlike them, he seemed to compensate for his size by eccentricities and a flamboyant personality. He wore a bow tie or a cravat, fastened with a gold pin.

Okay, and I wear butterflies on my dress and daisies on my shoes, so who am I to call the kettle black?

Gervie was nodding and Pip came smartly back to the present as he said, "I see. I understand perfectly how *you* are involved in *Delphine,* since it's your concept and mostly your choreography, but how does Mister Carpenter-Rivers come into the tale?"

Pip shrugged her shoulders to her ears. She had no clue how Humph had inserted himself into the world of her dolphins and treasure and dance.

Tamzin said, "We don't know either. He just popped up the other day and recorded the Tag tune while Costas was playing it. He transcribed it and gave it to me later. He said it was lucky I was holding my fiddle, or he might have given it to someone else. I have *no* idea what he meant by that."

Pip knew, but she decided not to mention it now—it would only confuse matters.

"Oh." Gervie sounded taken aback.

Tamzin said, gently, "I know it sounds chaotic, but honestly, Arts in Tune thrives on organised chaos. Matin and I agreed when we started all this that we'd let everyone keep their autonomy. We use a capsule system. *You* manage the Forever classes as you think best. If you'd prefer Quiff Man . . ." She glanced at Pip.

"Humph," Pip reminded.

"Okay. If you'd prefer Humph to back off and stick to the film, instead of transcribing music in his downtime, you should take it up with him. I know you'll do it with appropriate courtesy, and I would hope he'd receive it the same way.

After all, he might reasonably object if you stopped by to direct a scene or two of his film."

Gervie said, "I wouldn't stop him for the world. I simply wondered where he fitted into our equation."

"You know as much as I do," Tamzin said. She stretched. "I'm going for a break now. I have two equines, two dogs, and a daughter who'll be wondering where I am, and I'm wondering in turn where my husband is. Has anyone seen him lately?"

"He might be at the soundstage," Pip said.

"So he might. What's the time?"

"It's nearly five, Mistress Campania!" Jane called out from where she stood with Richenda. The girl seemed to have a clock in her head.

"That late? It'll have to be a *short* break. I guess I'll be seeing some of you for Dancing Down the Dusk in half an hour."

Various people called enthusiastic assent and walked away, presumably in search of a quick cup of something or other.

"The ideas I have . . ." Tamzin made a comical shrug and grinned at Pip. "I need my head read, but I seem to have a bit of a habit of jumping into things feet first and worrying about the state of my shoes later."

Pip, who was mostly the opposite, glanced at Tamzin's shoes. "Love those," she said, noticing rainbow-patterned heels on the sturdy but elegant footwear.

"So do I. Remind me to tell you how I came by them one day." Tamzin pointed one toe. "I wear these all the time to remind me I'm dancing on love."

With that poetic but rather peculiar statement, she turned and hurried off, presumably in search of her family.

Pip stood indecisively until Jane came over to her.

"Are you thrilled with your ballet, Miss Pip?"

"I am, rather," Pip admitted. "It's so much *bigger* than I

thought." She remembered she had Jane to thank that this was all happening *now* and on such a scale. "Jane, it was kind of you to suggest this to your aunt."

Jane widened her eyes. "Not at all! I knew she'd want to do it. Delphine is a beautiful part, and she'll *love* beguiling Corin away from his murderous tendencies."

"That's good then," Pip said. She was going to ask who Corin was, but she remembered in time that he was Richenda's fiancé, who would be dancing the seafay. She wondered if someone would paint him silver and green, and if he'd mind. Unlike the seafay man she'd seen in that brief, disturbing encounter *over there* with Tane, he would have to wear clothing. Maybe a full bodysuit in iridescent colours would do.

He'd need a name, too. She thought of the resounding nomenclatures of the sea fay she'd heard of . . . Lore Mor Arlodh, Mariner van der Strand and his wife Meribelle . . . and pondered her options.

"Phileas Tide," she decided aloud.

Jane gave her a startled look.

"That's a name for the seafay in the ballet."

"Oh! That sounds rather fine," Jane said. She turned to engage Pip's full attention. "How about the dolphin soloist? What will you call her?"

Pip pondered dolphin-style names. Then she recalled the slender Amalie with her tambourine-like instrument. "What's the name of the musical thing Amalie was playing?" she asked.

Jane clasped her hands. "It's a tamberchime. How *perfect!*"

Pip just hoped she could remember the names with it was time to tell Gervais.

Oh, wait—

She took her feint-ruled green pad out of her messenger bag, unclipped the pen, and wrote down the names. "Is there anyone else who needs naming?" she asked.

"Maybe Delphine needs a last name, since she's human," Jane suggested.

Pip nodded assent. "Something to do with dancing, or the sea. Or something . . . Um. Delphine Grey."

"That's so elegant," Jane said.

Pip thought so too, and she wrote it down.

"What did Gervie mean—auditions?" she asked as Jane ushered her towards the café area. "*Delphine* is already cast—isn't it?"

"This is not for *Delphine*. Richie told me it's something Master Almaclair calls *outreach* auditions. It's to let people who want to dance show what they can do . . . and to find out whether they have *potential*. I did know about it, but I hadn't realised it was formal."

"Are you going to audition?" Pip knew Jane hoped to join the Forever troupe at some stage.

Jane said, "I'd love to, and I long to, but I'm not good enough."

"You don't need to be *good enough* yet—surely. You need to show potential."

Jane said, gently, but with the steel Pip had occasionally seen in her, "I'm related to Richie. There *will* be comparisons. I have to be *good* before I try out. The way they say Amalie was. She had to be *so* good for Master Almaclair to take her."

Pip wondered what Amalie had to do with it. She pressed on, "You are already good for—"

"For a beginner. I know. Laura says that often. She says I'll be better than her, but she's not nearly as good as Richie or Amalie. She can teach me at present, but soon I'll need someone better—who knows more, I mean. Laura says that too, so it's not just me being over-ambitious. I need to practise a lot more, too."

Pip didn't understand exactly what was going on in Jane's

head, but she saw there would be no changing it, so she didn't try. Instead, she said, "Are you going to dance down the dusk?"

Jane nodded. She added, wistfully, "I wish I *was* good enough to dance in the *corps de ballet* in *Delphine.* I can do the dolphin steps, but I'm not ready."

"I'm not either," Pip said, and added, in her mind, *and unlike you, young Jane, I never will be.*

Jane brightened. "Never mind, I'll be in it one day. I'll choose a character name for myself, so I can learn how to *be* her. I think I'll be Waveweaver."

"Lovely," Pip said. She was pleased to see the mythology of *Delphine* growing without her input.

She remembered something. "Jane, did I ever tell you I was going to have a cat scene in *Delphine*?"

"I don't think so." Jane wrinkled her forehead. "How would cats fit in with underwater scenes?"

"I realised they wouldn't. That was at an early stage . . ."

They'd reached the café area by now and Pip saw, with relief, that they would have time to eat after all. The blond server was laying out platters of scones and sandwiches with fruit and pots of tea and coffee on a makeshift trestle table. Two blonde girls wearing what Pip thought were called dirndls were assisting, along with a dark, shadowy young man in Tyrolean dress and an apron.

"Do we just help ourselves?" she asked.

One of the dirndl girls said, "Please do, and eat lots. Yannick gets tetchy if no one eats his special scones." A flirtatious glance in the dark man's direction showed exactly who Yannick was.

"Yannick?" Pip queried as she picked up a small plate and started loading it.

Gones, she thought, remembering family-speak at the Delmsford Flower Show, back in February.

Jane said, "That's an alpenfee name, Miss Pip. If he was

courtfolk, he'd be called John or Jehan, and a braeman might be called Iain."

"I see." Pip wondered again about Jane's own name. A fairy called *Jane* didn't compute, especially when she considered Jane's highly individual parents. She added, "But I thought alpenfee people were *blond*."

"Some of them are, but not all, by any means. Like courtfolk. Amalie's pure court, but she has dark hair."

Pip said, hopefully, "Cambric tea?"

The second dirndl girl said, "The pot with the daisies. Are you Miss Pippin? Tamzin's friend? Dequan said you might want it, so he made that pot especially for you."

Pip and Jane moved back to eat and drink, and Jane said, "What were you saying about cats in the early stages of *Delphine*?"

Cats. Three pictures came into Pip's mind, clashing rather. First, she saw Kittisack and Amberjill, with Lupin's cat. She missed them sharply, along with the peace of Lemonwood Cottage. She hoped they were behaving well for Clarkia.

Sliding in front of them she saw the illustration Tamzin had been working on—a copy of a page in *Grandmother's Sunshine,* depicting three cats that resembled her housemates.

Finally, she saw a group of youthful cats, bouncing eagerly around an old queen.

She shook her head to clear it of the visions. "I meant there to be a transforming scene where the dolphins turned into cats and danced on land. There was going to be an old queen cat . . . but then I realised it didn't fit in the ballet as it developed."

"That's such a pity," Jane said, almost as Tamzin had. "It would have been fun."

"I think so too. I thought it would be something *I* could do with children. I could dance the old queen myself because it wouldn't matter if she wasn't especially skilled. She'd be a comedy character part."

Jane put down a scone and turned a hopeful face to Pip. "Maybe you could stage it with inexperienced dancers? Because cats are graceful, but they're funny too. They're a lovely mix of curves and angles, and fluff and bristles."

Pip thought of Amberjill, skittering after blowing leaves and wrestling clawfully with a lemon, and of the sleek Kittisack, who could sometimes be as elbowy as a dragon and as grumpy as nails on silk.

It *would* be fun.

What a pity she was so busy. What with the film, *Delphine* and all the other things she had to think of, she was busier than she'd been in years . . .

"Jane, would you like to work on that little scene with me while we're here?"

The words had popped out of her mouth, and she was aghast.

Jane said, as if reading her mind, "I'd *adore* it, Miss Pippin, but I can't see how you'd have the time . . . unless . . ." Her face lit up and she clasped her hands in her characteristic gesture of joy. "What if we use our morning practice time? We'd still be practising because— "

"Because what?" Pip felt forced to ask.

Jane spun herself in a pirouette.

"Because it can be done as a dancing class! The old queen is training the new generation in cat dance, and there's a young queen working *so* hard to make the old queen proud but tripping over a ball of wool and getting tangled!"

The sun was dropping, and sunset light slanted into Pip's eyes, dazzling her with the beautiful simplicity of Jane's suggestion. It was like being gifted a whole pristine hour of extra time.

We can round up Star and Laura and some of the other dawn and dusk dancers who aren't Forever *calibre . . . it can be our little project.*

She was drawing breath to answer Jane when she heard the cry of the fiddle.

Dancing Down the Dusk was about to begin.

Chapter Eight. I Need to Talk to the Cats

Pip made a new to-do list.

Magda had decided to have an early night, but before she settled to sleep she checked in with Pip.

"How are you managing, Pippin?"

"Managing?" Pip asked cautiously. She was busy with her list, which featured such things as Fay Spotting, *Queen of the Clowder*—ask Star, see if the dark boy—Tim?—will play, call Clarkia and check on the cats, find out who the fluting parson is, ask Jane about her name . . . Ask if that Dad would like to be a cat with boots on.

"Being back in the saddle," Magda clarified.

Pip had recently reacquainted herself with riding, with the friendly help of Jane's beau Ardal Cornfellow and an opinionated pony named Fimber, but she didn't think Magda was referring to that.

"Ah—"

Magda held her glass of whiskey to the light. There were a few sips left. She clarified again, saying, "I mean, it's been a long time since you worked. Are you finding it difficult? Are they expecting too much of you?"

"Not a bit," Pip said, surprised. "Didn't I tell you I just *do* it?"

"You did. And I must say you don't appear to be under stress when you're performing. On the other hand . . ." She paused, most uncharacteristically.

"What other hand?" Pip thought of Gervais Almaclair, who was lefthanded like Cousin Jan. He was *so* like an older version of Court Leopold, and also, from what she recalled, like a version of her old acting friend, Alain Barfleur.

But Alain was gentle and not so pleased with himself.

"I wonder if I could find *The House of Heriot* on E-Re," she added, following her train of thought.

"On what?" Magda sounded startled.

"E-Re."

"What the devil is that?"

Pip shrugged. She didn't know. It was just something she'd heard the Biblio-Reps mention.

Magda apparently gave up trying to follow. "What I was saying is, you don't seem to be acting up there, but on the other hand, you don't seem a bit like yourself."

"I told you. I don't act. I'm not an actor. I just do it. Be whoever I'm meant to be for as long as I need to be."

"I can't say I *see,* but if it works, it works. Jasper seems happy with your scenes."

"That's good," Pip said. She realised Magda wanted something more, so she added, "It's fine, I think. Humph wants to kill Mother to tolling bells or a tuning fork, but it will be offstage in any case and nothing to do with me. I told him to talk it over with Jasper."

Magda finished her whiskey with a single controlled gulp. She glanced at the bottle, shook her head, and went through her evening ritual of putting bottle and rinsed glass away in her case.

"I'm glad everything is working from your point of view," she said. "I'm turning in now, but there's no need to try to be quiet. I'm good at sleeping."

"Goodnight," Pip said. She wondered if Magda felt overwhelmed by everything that was going on. She didn't show it. "Did you know there was an alpenfee man serving afternoon tea today? He has dark hair, and his name is Yannick."

"No, I didn't." Magda rolled onto her side. She didn't sound very interested.

Pip reflected that she probably wasn't. Why should she be? Would *she* be interested if Magda had told her there was a fair-haired human man named Dequan serving a meal? What sort of a name was *Dequan*, anyway? French?

Must ask Tamzin. She'll know.

It was surprisingly easy to think of Tamzin as Tamzin. Pip knew she had once been Angie Blake, but although she occasionally caught a flash of the child she had known, Tamzin's memories of that time were necessarily hazy.

She's lived so much more than I have since then . . . She's spent years becoming Tamzin. I've spent decades being tiny Pippin Pearmain.

She worked on her Fay-Spotting list for a few minutes, putting down the examples she was sure of first.

Tane Pendennis—pisky-water halfling.

Jane Pendennis—pisky-water-human and probably sylvan mix.

She hesitated as she considered adding Ardal Cornfellow. She knew he was a hob, but she decided he didn't qualify as she hadn't seen him at the festival. Bother. That put Jillian Jules out of court, as well as the rest of the fossmere family.

Liffey Rosheen—leprechaun

Mull St Ives—pisky

Richenda—pisky-human halfling

Court Leopold—courtfolk

Tansy Leopold—hob

Gervais Almaclair—courtfolk

Hamish Almaclair—braefolk

Amalie—courtfolk . . . what's her last name?

Tim . . . whatever. Court quarterling with some pixie and human

Matin Campania—elf

Asher and Jessie —elves . . . last names?

Costas Capricorn—herdfee

Yannick—alpenfee . . . last name?

She wondered if the girls in dirndls were also alpenfee. She'd have to ask Jane, but she didn't know their names, so she couldn't properly add them. She'd already stretched a point with Amalie's young man. Okay, she'd made the rules, and she had only herself to blame if they were constrictive. There was no changing them now.

She had a total of fifteen names on her initial list. She supposed she could include baby Music and Jane's cousin Laura who was at least part pisky, but even that would bring the total to just seventeen.

It was quite a few, but when she considered the hundreds of people she'd seen over the past two days she saw it wasn't a significant number.

Magda was probably right. Most people here at Dance in Tune were as human as she was.

Oh! Magda was a little bit alpenfee and sylvan. Magda could be added.

Pip put her in and set aside her list. Tomorrow, she'd copy it onto a new page and put it in alphabetical order, leaving room for new entries as she found them. Mim, for example . . . what was she? She *looked* human, but so did most of them.

Magda appeared to be asleep, so Pip embarked on another item on her to-do list.

She called Clarkia.

"Hello? Pip?" Her cousin answered on the fourth ring.

"Yes, it's me. How is everything?"

Clarkia said, "Fine, I think. It's been quiet. I really like it here."

"Good. So do I." Pip felt a new rush of homesickness.

"I've been out in the garden, doing some reading for work—and I've also been reading some of your books. I went down to the café for lunch, just for fun. I got a tart with cream cheese in it. Pure indulgence."

"I'm glad you're comfortable," Pip said. It was a wee bit disturbing, thinking of someone else in her cottage, doing what she did. Oddly, she hadn't felt this way regarding Jamie when he looked after the cottage and cats. Maybe it was because Clarkia was a relation. "Are the cats there?" she asked.

"Yes. Kittisack is squatting at my feet. He looks as if he's plotting world domination."

"That sounds normal."

"Really? He seems to do it a lot."

"Don't worry about it unless he starts holding your ankles to ransom."

"Oh dear. Is that likely?"

"Probably not. I think he only does that to me. Maybe."

There was a small pause. Then Pip said, "Amberjill?"

"Oh, she's hiding in a cereal box. I don't know how she fits, but she manages. I can just see the tip of her tail."

That was new, but it didn't sound too terrible. "Lupin's cat?"

"You mean that—um—figurine Aunt Lupin made? It's okay. The cats seem to like schmoozing it for some reason. I checked in case it had a vent stuffed with catnip, but it hasn't. And how do they get on the mantelpiece?"

"Who knows how those two do anything? But that's normal, too—for them. Just wipe it over with a cloth if it gets too slobbered-upon. How's Bill?"

"He's good too."

"And my camomile?"

"It's fine. Plenty of bees."

Clarkia sounded a bit too patient, and Pip thought she must be afraid they'd go through every plant and creature at Lemonwood Cottage.

She was tempted to see how far she could push it, but she cut short the catechism in the interests of family harmony. "It sounds as if you're all okay, then."

"Yes, thanks." Clarkia seemed about to hang up, so Pip pressed on.

"Clarkia, there was something I wanted to ask you and your mum. I was going to wait until I get home, but now I have you on the line—"

Clarkia broke in. "Actually, Mum's here too. We thought it would be okay."

"It's fine. Even better because I can talk to you both at once instead of making two calls or getting one of you to relay information and questions to the other. Can you put your phone on speaker?"

"She already did." Jan's voice sounded a little distant, but definitely amused. "Is that film happening now or later?"

"Now. I'll tell you about it when I come home. I have a couple of things I wanted to run by you two now though."

"We're all ears," Jan said.

"All right. The first one is *Grandmother's Sunshine.*"

"What of it?" Jan asked warily.

"Remember, you and I were discussing it the day you came to visit? The day you brought me the envelopes and Lupin's cat?"

"Yes."

"We were talking about Callie and Cammie, the girls who have their names in the books."

"That's right," Jan said.

Clarkia put in, "Mum told me you were interested in genealogy, Pip. I have some information on the family, but it's not very substantial. I don't suppose you're interested in Dad's side, or even in Grandad de Leon."

Pip wasn't, very, but she murmured politely.

"I did go back a bit in Great-Nanna Laurel's ancestry, and that's the line that pertains to the books," Clarkia went on. "I was looking at Callie, because she's our direct-line ancestor."

"Ja? Und?" Pip got up from the bed where she'd been sitting and bounced on her toes.

Clarkia laughed. "Goodness, you sound just like Aunt Lupin when you say that! Anyway, I am pretty sure Callie was Calanthe Darby. Her married name was Godsell—her husband was Richard Godsell. They married in eighteen twenty."

"What do you mean *pretty sure*?" Pip enquired.

"Just what I said. Going back that far is a matter of matching birth records with dates, parents' names, and marriages, then reading between the lines and filling gaps with newspaper archives, wills and obituaries, sailing dates, and so forth."

"Oh." Pip felt chastened. "Sailing?"

"They weren't born in Australia. Lincolnshire seems the most likely option. Sometimes, not every child of a marriage is listed. Some children were just put down as *Baby Darby* or *F Darby* or some such—I did think that meant a name such as Fanny or Frederick, but then I realised it just stands for *female*. Get three of those in a family and you're pretty much stuffed as to how they connect or what their names were.

"Say Annie Darby marries in 1845 . . . how can you know if she is the F born in 1821, or one of the later ones? Then, Susan Brown leaves a legacy to *my dear son Justin*, but there's no record of her ever having a son—and it turns out her cousin Clara had a nineth son and named him Justin, but he stopped being counted at her address in the census in the eighteen nineties. The supposition then is that Susan informally adopted him, so he became her nephew *and* her son—"

"Wait—who is Susan Brown?" Pip asked. She had no hope of keeping up now that Clarkia was in full flow.

"No one. Well, she was someone in Riley's family tree . . ." Clarkia's voice trailed away, and Pip tried, and failed, to identify anyone called Riley. Maybe he was Clarkia's ex-partner, with whom she had broken up when she discovered the ex-girlfriend and largely unknown children he'd mentioned were in fact both current and expecting him home from his *work travels.*

"Who is Annie Darby?"

"A fictional example," Clarkia said.

Jan said, "I think Clarkia is saying she is as sure as she can be that this Calanthe Darby who married Richard Godsell in eighteen twenty is Nanna Laurel's great-grandmother. Her son was possibly named Har, but that is probably a diminutive for something else. Best guess is Harold."

"You sound as if you've been studying up on this," Pip said.

"I read Clarkia's notes in case you asked. Har Godsell would be Nanna's grandfather."

Harold? Harley? Harvey? Hardy?

Clarkia took over again. "Was this what you rang to say?"

"Not exactly. It was more about the books than the people."

"Oh."

"It's very interesting though, and I do want to see it when I come home," Pip said in haste.

She did, too. Seeing it written down would make it easier to understand. With Jan and Clarkia detailing it over the phone, she couldn't get a grip on it.

"What about the books?" Jan asked.

Pip drew in a deep breath. It seemed less of a good idea to broach this on the phone now she was on the point of doing it. "Magda—my agent—was interested in them," she explained.

"That's who you wanted the photos for," Clarkia said.

"Yes. She has an art gallery in Western Australia. But it's not only Magda. Jan, I don't know if you remember, or even if you ever knew, but twenty-five years or so ago I used to teach dancing to playgroup children. Informally, I mean."

"I don't think I ever knew that," Jan said.

"Well, it doesn't matter. You would have been too busy

with work and looking after Clarkia to care what I was up to. The point is, I used to mind one of the children sometimes." It occurred to Pip that this was less than tactful. She had never offered to mind Clarkia. Not that Jan had ever asked.

Pip pressed on, "She liked stories, and I used to read to her."

"And I'm guessing you read *Grandmother's Sunshine,*" Jan said.

"I did." Pip edited out Tamzin's childhood name changes, the family's flit and her own one-time impulse to give away her copy of the book. She continued smoothly, "She loved the stories. And guess what?"

There was silence from her cousins.

Pip said, "I just met that little girl again. I wouldn't have recognised her, but she's an artist now and she was drawing one of the pictures from *Grandmother's Sunshine.*"

"Copying, you mean?" Jan sounded a bit censorious.

"Not exactly."

Clarkia said, "Do you mean she has a copy of that book herself?"

"She told me she has tried to buy it, but she can't find any copies, or even any proof it ever existed. She has a baby girl, so she was drawing one of the pictures from memory. It's *my* copy of the book she remembers. She's never seen another one."

The silence that greeted this was somehow disconcerted.

Then Jan said, carefully, "Are you saying you want to sell, or give, your copy to this girl?"

"It's *your* copy, so you can do as you like with it," Clarkia said reasonably. "You don't have to ask *our* permission."

"No-o, but I promised your mum just recently that I'd mention it to her if I ever wanted to sell. First refusal—though it would be a gift. And anyway, I don't want to sell. I want to keep it in the family. It's just pure coincidence that I ran into my old friend again. Her name is Tamzin, by the way."

"What are you thinking of, then?" Jan asked.

"I wondered if we might have new copies made. Either just a few, privately printed, or else actually published for general sale."

"Can you do that?" Clarkia asked.

"It could be done, by scanning the pages, but as for whether we're *allowed* to do it, I think we probably are. There's no author or illustrator name anywhere in the book and Magda, my agent, is quite an expert on Victorian children's illustrators. She didn't recognise the pictures and she says with an illustrator that good, she should have done. Mind you, I should think they're *pre*-Victorian if that marriage date you gave for Callie is right."

"George the third, I should think—maybe Regency period," Jan put in.

Pip said, "There seem to be no other copies listed anywhere, so what does that look like?"

"It looks like a private and highly limited printing," Jan said. She added, reflectively, "It's those gravestones all over again, Clarkia. It would be *so* useful if they'd say Harold Godsell, son of, grandson of, husband of, father of . . . and chisel in all the dates. Instead of that, his stone has *Har. Godsell. At rest*. It ought to add, *under the lichen,* because we had to chip away forests of the stuff to read even that much."

She added, "It would also be so useful if Grandmother Aster had happened to put, *For darling Calanthe Darby . . . this book is one I made and printed especially for you in the year . . .* or something like that, then written her own name. I mean, she calls herself Grandmother Aster. Is that her first name or her surname?"

Pip said, "If we have the only two copies, and if it *is* a private printing, I suppose we can bring out a new edition, if we choose."

Jan said, "I could run it past the lovely Hot Unicorns."

"Come on, Ma, it's not in their line," Clarkia said, laughing.

Considering Hot Unicorn Press published the saucy mystery novels Jan wrote under her Juniper Gin pen name, Pip agreed with Clarkia's summation.

"I'm sure you're right, but I can ask them to walk me through the ins and outs of it," Jan said. She added, "What would our purpose be, though? It wouldn't be a profitable enterprise. We'd have to pay for printing, I should think, and colour printing in limited editions costs two arms and a leg."

"I wasn't thinking of profit. I just thought it would be nice if Tamzin could have a copy for her little girl. And Magda would *love* to display the artwork in her gallery. She might sell prints, and I expect we could come to some financial arrangement, since the material copies belong to us. I mean, they might be public domain, but we aren't obligated to hand them over to anyone. If we *did* copy them, I think anyone who bought a copy could make more, but that's not really the point."

Her cousins were silent, possibly exchanging glances or thinking.

Pip said, "I decided I'd run it past you, to see what you thought."

"Your copy is *yours,*" Clarkia said again.

"I know, but it's a family heirloom too. If copies were made of mine, even if no one else made third generation copies, it would reduce the rarity value of yours. If one of us had, say, Callie's wedding ring, I should think we'd all want to agree on selling it . . . or not, or having several copies made, or not."

"Lupin had some jewellery that belonged to Nanna Laurel's mother," Jan said.

"Oh?"

"Nothing valuable. Just something that came to her as the eldest of us. It jumped Mum and Aunt Rosie because—"

Because no one ever quite knew which one was older.

Pip didn't like to ask what had become of the jewellery, but Jan said, "Lupin left it to me, but now I come to think of it, you're the eldest now. Maybe—"

"No! I'd like to see it one day, but I'm not really a jewellery person. Remember all those seed-pearl bracelets the studio insisted on giving me?"

"God yes!" Jan giggled. "And the plush cats with diamanté collars . . . You gave me some of them for Clarkia when she was born."

"What? I don't remember that!" Clarkia said.

"No, you wouldn't. You were such a dribbly baby. I put them away until you were old enough to play with them sensibly instead of teething on the collars."

"I should remember them, then."

"I sort of forgot to get them out. They're still in the attic, somewhere, if you want them."

"I'd at least like to see them, so I can thank Pip properly for the thoughtful gift," Clarkia said with mock reproach.

Pip had no memory of giving the cats to Clarkia. She wondered if she had really done it, or if Little Mum or one of the Little Nannas had thought it would be a nice idea and given them to Jan in her name. If so, it seemed to have backfired.

She shrugged, although of course they couldn't see her. "You probably didn't miss much, Clarkia. They weren't exactly my thing. I collect stuff, but it's stuff I like, not random plush—" She wound down.

"If you're sure about the jewellery . . ." Jan ventured.

"I'm sure. But as for the books, could you ask your Hot Unicorns? If they say it's plausible, and if you two don't mind, I could mention it to Tamzin and Magda." *And to Jonquil Orange . . . who tried to persuade me* and *Tamzin that the book never existed.*

Pip liked Jonquil, but the thought of proving the expert *wrong* rather pleased her. It would be mean, but wouldn't the meanness be balanced by allowing Jonquil a way to give those occasional clients what they asked for?

"I'll give them a call tomorrow," Jan said. "Is that all?"

"No, there's something else. I know this is going to sound weird, but I need to talk to the cats."

Chapter Nine. Cat-Morse on the Line

"You're right. It does sound weird," Jan said, but she sounded as if she was smiling. "Clarkia, is Unseelie still under the table?"

Unseelie was the name Jan called Kittisack. It somewhat suited him.

"He's here," Clarkia's voice reported.

"Ask him if he wants to talk to Pip."

"Unseelie, do you—"

Pip sighed loudly. Jan and Lupin had made a grand double act. Clearly, Clarkia was a capable replacement for her aunt.

"Sorrow." Jan, quoting a childhood book, didn't sound repentant. She paused, then said, "Cat on the line. Do you want us to give you some privacy?"

"Suit yourselves," Pip said. "Kittisack?"

She had no idea if he would answer, but he did. He normally communicated in visual Cat-Morse, but because Pip couldn't see him, this time it was mind-to-mind.

Tell no one.

"It's a bit late for that. Kittisack, how are you getting on with Clarkia and Jan?"

They are mostly respectful, and Clarkia provides food in good quantity and good flavour. She is a little less than generous with the cheese.

"So am I, according to you. And Amberjill complained about Jamie's cheese production too. No actual problems, though, other than greed?"

We told you we would be well-provided for with Clarkia.

Pip identified Amberjill's gentler tones. Maybe she'd come out of the cereal box.

"I know. I'm glad. Is Lupin's cat still watching over you?"

He is, he has been, and he will be.

"Good. Try to keep the slobber to a minimum. I'm sure Clarkia has better things to do than to wipe cat-dribble off pottery household cat gods. Kittisack—"

Address me as the original cat.

"Trust you to be awkward. *Original cat,* then, do you remember Kakao? He—"

I remember that fine dog. He and I bonded over adding nitrogen to the lemon tree.

Pip had a sudden mind picture of a chocolate brown poodle with his leg cocked and a Siamese tom with an upright trembling tail as they watered the evil-minded sentient lemon in her garden. She bit her lip.

What of him? Is he coming back?

Did Kittisack sound hopeful?

"Do you want him to?" she asked.

We have no quarrel with Kakao. He is a respectful beast who knows his place.

Kakao wasn't precisely a beast, being the mutable manifestation self of Jamie Pendennis who was Laura's brother and Jane's cousin, but Pip let it go.

She went on, "A person named Gillan has offered me a fay puppy to adopt. If I agree, it will come home to live with us. I will try to communicate with it in Dog-Morse."

Tell no one.

"For heaven's sake, Kitti—original cat! What sort of answer is that?"

Pip was sure she detected a cattish snigger.

What manner of fay puppy? Amberjill asked. Pip remembered she had been less than willing to countenance the advent of Lupin's cat until she understood it was not made of flesh and fur.

She said, soothingly, "Gillan said there are harlequins, that are small, and hollies, that are quiet, and heather hoonds that are bouncy, and shadowhonds that are even quieter than hollies."

She waited without much hope for their reply, but instead, she became aware they were discussing the matter. What was more, they were discussing it on a Cat-Morse party line, so she could get the sense of it.

They were not in favour of a heather hoond. Kittisack thought a harlequin would be a pleasing addition to the household, as it might be small enough to be dominated. Amberjill preferred the idea of a holly. How either of them knew what such dogs were like, Pip had no clue. She was pretty sure there were no fay dogs in Jellico Bay. Or—maybe? Until recently she hadn't known fay dogs existed. The bay could be swarming with the creatures for all she knew.

She waited while the discussion Cat-Morsed back and forth. Finally, Kittisack addressed her directly.

Tell no one. But if you decide to do this, I suggest you research what the back-up cat would prefer.

"Oh?" It was unlike Kittisack to take much notice of Amberjill, let alone to defer to her preferences.

My remaining span is less than hers. Therefore, it makes sense that she will cohabit longer with the beast than I.

"Are you—"

I am perfectly well. I have a goodly time remaining. It is simply less than the back-up cat has because she has less time behind her.

Pip supposed that made sense. "What, then? Amberjill?"

A shadowhond would be a pleasant idea, the back-up cat suggested. She sent Pip a mind picture of a round black hummock of a dog with a small calico cat curled on top as if on a hassock.

Well! Amberjill expected to use the puppy as a bed.

Pip felt a touch of excitement. This might really happen!

Her fingers found the promise blank bracelet Gillan had given her.

It was the first jewellery she had worn in a long while, discounting the brief time she'd worn the resized heaven and earth ring before she left it behind in the fossmere cave.

"You wouldn't be horrible to it, would you?"

Noooo.

Would we do that?

Hmm. That didn't sound encouraging.

Another Cat-Morse message came on the line, this time from Lupin's cat.

Mistress, I will ensure my dear children are not unkind to anyone under this roof. There was a little pause before it added, *Or in the garden.*

"Thank you!"

Pip beamed. "One more question. Bitch or dog?"

Gillan had recommended a bitch, but a dog could join forces with Kittisack to keep the lemon tree supplied with nitrogen and balance the household.

Dog, came the emphatic chorus.

Kittisack tossed her a mind picture of Kakao. They *liked* Kakao. They wanted one with a cocky leg like him.

"Thank you!" Pip said again. Then she said, "Can you get Jan and Clarkia to come back?"

Jan said, in a choked voice, "We never went away."

There was a gasp, another choke and a sudden gust of laughter from Pip's cousins.

She frowned, then shrugged.

"Ja? *Und*?" she said ferociously.

Clarkia spluttered.

"How much did you get from that?" Pip asked.

"You're getting a dog?" Jan sounded as if she was suppressing more laughter.

"Yes. Probably. But I had to clear it with the cats, and with you. Clarkia, if I do get a pup, will you be willing to look after it if I have to go away for work again?"

Clarkia made a choking noise.

Jan said, "That was a yes. Pip, Clarkia will be happy to look after your cats, your cottage, your dog, or whatever, although she would probably draw the line at another vicious gooseberry bush unless you provide her with a machete for self-defence. If, for any reason, she can't be here, I will sub for her. Okay?"

Pip blew her cheeks out. "Okay. I'd better go. I have another call to make. Goodnight."

"Goodnight," her cousins said in chorus.

Vaguely, in the background, Kittisack could be heard to say, *Tell no one.*

Chapter Ten. The Promise Blank

Pip, intent on striking while the opportunity was hot, dug out the card Gillan St Ives had given her.

She considered email, but opted for the more direct route, calling Gillan's personal number.

It rang a few times before a somewhat exasperated voice said, "Yes?"

That didn't sound promising. Pip wondered what the time was. Maybe it was too late to be calling people she barely knew.

She said, "This is Pippin Pearmain . . . Marigold Heriot. From *The House of Heriot.* Remember?"

"Yes, of course. My son said you'd shown up at Dance in Tune. You're filming there?"

"That's right. I've thought your offer over, and I'd like to take you up on it."

"You'd like a puppy."

"Yes. If that's still all right."

"Certainly. I don't make offers I don't intend to carry through on."

Just like Magda, then.

Suddenly suspicious, she glanced at the second bed, but her agent seemed utterly relaxed.

Gillan went on, "Have you decided on the type?"

"I'd like a shadowhond. And can it be a dog? I know you said a bitch, but—"

"It's better to go with what you want rather than what *I* recommend," Gillan said. She sounded more friendly. "I did get in touch with some people who have breeding pairs, and you're in luck. Fay dogs don't tend to large litters, so I put your name down provisionally. I'll confirm it with the shadow breeder *now.*"

"Thank you. Do I need to be inspected, or anything?"

Gillan seemed to be considering. "Generally . . . but you live with fay cats which actually communicate with you. Would *they* recommend you?"

Pip explained that the cats had liked Kakao and that they seemed cognisant with the various types of fay dog. "They decided on a shadow dog."

"But what did *you* decide on?"

"I let them have the say, since it's their house too."

"Then I'm sure you need not be inspected."

"Good. I also have the word of a—a kind of guardian—that they won't be unkind to it, although Amberjill does intend to use it as a pillow."

Gillan laughed. "That might be interesting! Right, then, I'll put this deal in motion. I'll be in touch when the litter is born, and I'll see that you're kept up to date on its progress. If there is more than one dog in the litter, there might even be a choice."

"Can I have the number of the people directly? I could have photos emailed."

"No. That is, she doesn't have a number. She lives *over there.* Most breeders do."

"I *see.* Will the pup be all right without other fay dogs around?"

"Yes—it will have the cats, and you. It will also interact quite happily with standard dogs—or muties, come to that. They're adaptable beasts—and pack animals. They make a pack from whoever is available."

"Will I be able to pick out a name, or will it have one already?"

Again Gillan seemed to be considering. "That's difficult to say. Fay beasts sometimes have their own notions of naming. What often happens is that the breeders let prospective companions know the family names, and something emerges from that. Or, sometimes serendipity takes centre stage."

Pip nodded, although Gillan couldn't see her. That was what happened in her family. Her grandmothers had both had floral names, and so had her mother and aunt. Her dad, coincidentally, had an apple name. All these considerations had led to her name and her cousins', even as far as Clarkia. Jan had been *so* proud of herself to have come up with a floral name that paid rhyming tribute to Clarkia's father, Mark.

"I'll wait and see then," she said.

"That's the best course," Gillan said. "Is it a deal? You are committed to giving a shadow dog a home, caring for him, and working to communicate with him at the same level you use with the cats? You will be his companion, and he will be yours, whether or not the communication works as you intend."

That had the sound of a contract.

"Yes. I'm committed."

Pip, who almost never committed to anything other than work, felt nothing but pleased excitement.

"And *I* am committed to facilitating the acquisition and delivery at no cost to you. I would like to know what happens with the Dog-Morse project, but that is not a requirement of the deal."

Pip said, "This is the point where we should shake hands, or something."

"Or something," Gillan said. "Let's take it as done. I'll shake my own hands and you do yours."

That suited Pip perfectly. She said so and hung up.

Having dealt with what she could for the day, she stepped into the minute bathroom, shed her festival dress, and inspected it. She'd been dancing, eating, and socialising in it for a couple of days, and it had spent quite a few hours draped over a rail in the dressing room while Pip wore Solace's overalls on set. She'd dropped it on over a face still lightly made up with Solace's translucent pallor and sat around in it on the grass while she ate her al fresco meals. It was surely due for a rinse through at the least.

She gave it a snapping shake and another critical stare. Not a mark, not a smudge, not a crease. She sniffed it suspiciously, but all she smelled was a slightly fresh scent, reminiscent of newly-mown grass.

To wash or not to wash?

Pip weighed the light, silky garment in her right hand, tossed it to her left, played eeny-meeny, and laid it over the small stool in the corner. No point in washing what wasn't stained, smelly, or grubby.

She decided her lacy bra could survive another day, peeled off her wispy knickers and stepped into the shower with her favourite Caraway's Comforts soap. She and the knickers would shower together. She could air dry them overnight.

If I wore old-lady pants that came up to my chin they'd still be damp in the morning, she thought smugly. As it is . . . they'll be dry before I am, almost. Ergo, sage-green Wispy Knickers is an intelligent choice.

Ouch. She'd snagged her shoulder on the spigot. Smugness at her own intelligence never went unpunished.

She let the water mantle her shoulders, rubbing the small scrape and wishing she was back at the fossmere. She didn't often wish to be somewhere else, or with someone else, because her life was a product of her choice to surround herself with things she loved plus a couple she didn't, just for variety, and the company of cats.

Maybe I'll want something else when I grow up, she mused. She knew how ridiculous this was.

Maybe I'm in the process of growing up now.

Aware it was getting late, she spent less time in the shower than she wanted, dried herself, hung out the knickers, and turned to put on the long T-shirt she wore to bed. As she pushed her arms through it, her bracelet caught, pulling tight against her skin.

Half in and half out of the shirt, Pip paused to disentangle the silver cord. It came free, and she pushed it back into position around her left wrist.

Gillan had given it to her in the hamper of treats as a rather over-the-top peace offering after their chilly first encounter at the Fairy Gardens.

Tane Pendennis, who came from a family of silversmiths and jewellers, had identified the charm as a piece his father Merryn had made. He'd called it a *promise blank* and said it would draw, or summon, someone or something to her.

It was doing its job. Even now a tiny scrap was developing inside a shadow bitch *over there.* He might be no bigger than her thumb as yet, but one day he would come to live with her and the cats.

And he won't be an experiment. He will be a friend for us all.

Pip pictured her pup. She knew he wasn't born yet, and even when he was he would be a smudgy pup-shaped blob for a while, unable to stand or see. She seemed to recall that pups could leave their mothers at seven or eight weeks or so, but he'd have to come to her by boat or plane, so maybe he'd have to be a bit older than that.

Three months or more seemed a long time to wait for her new friend. A quarter of a year. She hummed as she tried to work out what percentage that was of her lifetime to date.

Multiply 66 by four . . . is that right?

Stop that.

She settled the bracelet and froze as she looked at the silver charm. She was sure it had been in the generic shape of a pup—beautifully made, but still an outline such as one might use as a stencil to colour in. Now it had altered in shape, so it looked more like an individual dog.

Moreover, it was less bright in colour. It looked to be turning black.

Pip rubbed it suspiciously with her thumb, but the dark stain remained.

It reminded her of the black stone in her heaven and earth ring, currently resting in the waterfall cave at the fossmere. That stone was a tektite.

Silver tarnishes, but not this soon, surely.

No. Not tarnish. It's turning tektite black.

Pip knew with certainty that her pup would be coming to her. She also knew what name he would have.

She remembered the pretty salutation Jane's family sometimes used.

Greet you, Tektite. Welcome to my world, to my heart, and to the company of cats.

Chapter Eleven. Cat Ballet

In no time, it seemed, Pip was dancing in the dawn with the rest of the festival.

The music ceased at six and Tamzin called out that she would see them all again in the evening to dance down the dusk. Pip recalled she had things to ask Tamzin, and probably to tell her, but this morning her old friend didn't linger to socialise with the festival-goers. Instead, she went off immediately with Matin and their daughter and, Pip noted with a new and proprietary interest, a couple of dogs. One was sort of a terrier-type with a curved tail, and the other was wholly a Pekingese. The almost-terrier capered and bounced and flounced her tail while the obvious peke trundled along with a rolling gait and a glistening cape of fur. The peke's gaze seemed drawn to a stuffed toy of some kind dangling from Matin's belt. Pip wondered if it belonged to the dog or to the child or even, conceivably, to both.

An unbelievably small pony joined them at a canter—so small Pip thought for a moment it was another dog. Its ears jammed back, and it aimed a playful nip at the terrier.

Pip *hoped* it was playful.

It must have been, because Matin, who was carrying his daughter, stilled the pony with a hand to its neck and set the child astride. Music hung on to the tufted mane and expressed her determination to *go-go-go.*

Well, Tamzin had mentioned she had animals.

With the goats added in and another pony—or was it a horse—somewhere or other there was quite a menagerie on the island.

Pip hurried off to find breakfast, which she ate on the move. Practice wasn't until seven, but she had to find Jane and rustle up someone to play music.

A stocky shape loomed up, surrounded by goats.

Perfect.

Pip noted in parentheses that this was probably why the goats had been absent from the family group.

"Master Capricorn? Greet you!"

The herdfee paused. "Mistress Pippin?"

"Just Pip will do."

"Then call me Costas. What can I do for you?"

"Do you know Jane?"

"Is that the enthusiastic maid who dances with you in the mornings and organises folk into doing things they didn't intend by sheer force of her wish that they should do them? *That* Jane?"

That sounded like the right Jane, so Pip nodded.

"Yes. Jane and I want to work on a ballet."

"But—"

"Not *Delphine*. The *Forevers* are doing that. This is a cat ballet."

"A second ballet!" He sounded pleased.

"Yes, but this is a little private project we would like to do in the mornings."

"And you would like cat music."

Pip looked up at him hopefully. "Would you? If you're too busy . . ."

"I would and I will. Can Mim come too? Or is it this a secret?"

"Mim the spinet player with the pretty smile?"

He nodded. "She plays the piccolo as well as the spinet and she likes cats."

"She can join in if she likes," Pip said magnanimously.

"Where and when?"

"The barn?" she suggested. "Soon?"

Costas pushed a couple of questing goat noses out of the way and reached in his bag for gingerbread. "We'll be there."

Having arranged her music and venue, Pip realised she still had to find Jane. She thought Star might like to come too and remembered she had not yet got her contact details regarding the tulip escapade they planned.

She was still puzzling over that when she saw Laura Pendennis and hurried to intercept her. "Laura, do you know where Jane is?"

"Not exactly," Laura said, "but I should think she's looking for you. She's been bubbling at me half the night about cat ballet. My ears are buzzing."

"Sorry."

Laura rolled her eyes. "No need to be sorry, Pip—you are called Pip, right? The same Pip my brother flummoxed by turning into a dog?" She laughed suddenly. "He took his dog basket to your place. I mean . . . how weird must that be on a scale of one to ten to the uninitiated?"

"About nine and a half and yes, that's me. Only I'm a bit more initiated now. And there are much worse things a young man can do than turn into a dog . . . especially a charming dog such as Kakao." Pip looked at Laura with interest. "Do you have a dog self too?"

"Regrettably, no. I have a fiancé, but not a dog self."

"Why?"

"Why the fiancé or why not the dog?"

"The dog."

"I don't know. Mutie-dogs are more common in men, I suppose. Jamie and Dad and Grandad Pendennis all dog out with disconcerting regularity, but *I* can't. Grandma Rachel can't, but she's human. Mum can't either, but then she doesn't have any pisky blood. I have just as much as Jamie, so—" She shrugged. "Yet no dog-self. Not yet, anyway. Maybe I just haven't discovered the way to unleash it. Her. If Jamie hadn't been messing round with semaphore then he wouldn't have found out either, unless he had happened to take up an occupation that meant he had to salute someone." Laura snapped a swift salute, stood on one leg and rubbed her foot on her calf, and raised her other hand.

Pip chuckled. "You look like one of those Indian god statues with all the arms and legs. Durga . . . Vishnu . . . Shiva . . ."

Laura resumed her normal stance. "No dog. Maybe I have to touch my tongue to my left elbow or something like that."

"Never mind. You have a fiancé."

Laura brightened. "I do. If he was here, I'd present him to be admired, but he's at work. I miss him, even with all this going on." She swept her arm around. "He does a marvellous belly rub. Um . . . maybe I *do* have an inner dog."

Pip tactfully ignored that. "Are you joining us for cat ballet?"

"Of course, if you'll have me. Jane seemed to think it would be okay."

Pip thought Laura seemed reassuringly normal, possible inner dog notwithstanding, so she asked her a question that had been tugging at her mind for days. "Why is Jane called Jane?"

"Why is Jane called Jane? Same reason I'm called Laura. It's her name."

"But *why*? Why *Jane*? She's a fairy."

"I know," Laura said patiently. "She's my little cousin and I love her, but she is most definitely a fairy. There's some human lurking in her DNA courtesy of Grandma Zena—that's Jill's mum—but you'd need a microscope to find it." She pointed at herself. "Now, *I* am half human through Grandma Rachel and Grandma Mary. Grandfather Cottman is a hob and Grandad Pendennis is a pisky. You don't see me jingling with a hundredweight of silver or wandering round in a cambric marquee and six petticoats. I don't even have very pointed ears."

"No," Pip observed.

"Bog standard human, from all appearances."

Pip knew a slippery declaration when she heard one. *I bet you're not. Dog or no dog.*

"So—what's your fiancé?"

"Drop dead gorgeous. Sandy hair and brown eyes. Smells of feijoas. Dependable. Wants *me* or no one."

"Yes, but—"

"His dad is a lovely human man with a beard—he looks like a tidy Viking. His mum is a devious pisky minx who is all tawny kitty-cat with steely eyes and not a bit pleased with me for nabbing her darling youngest. Fortunately, Louise and Illya paved the way by appropriating Marsh brothers one and two, though not in that order." She chuckled. "Illya's human and Louise is just a little bit pisky. *I,* on the other hand, am a halfling with precisely as much fay blood as Caden. It doesn't show, but it's there. My pisky percentage is lower, but I have a nice quarter of hob, so Keeley Marsh can put that in her pipe and smoke it. She can't possibly object to human blood, since she married Drew. Mind, she's mellowed a wee bit since Kerria was born. Illya put it to her straight—play nice and Kerria will be brought up loving Granny Marsh. Play passive aggressive and Kerria will be brought up being polite to Granny Marsh."

Pip decided she liked Laura a lot. "So, why is Jane called Jane?"

"Persistent, aren't you?"

"Very," Pip said.

"Okaaay, it goes like this." Laura started making points on her fingers. "First exhibit, Tane. You know him, or course. He caused a rumpus by jumping overboard, prompting you to call triple zero. Tane is my half uncle, and as mad as they come. He and Dad share lovely Grandad Pendennis, but Tane's mum is—"

"Mama Tam. I know her."

"Good. We all love Mama Tam. Tane was born by arrangement. Mama Tam went hunting for a lovely baby-daddy and found Grandad Pendennis who really is lovely, even if he's as nuts as Uncle Tane. It was all her idea, although he was happy to go along with it, so Mama Tam had the naming of the baby. She gave him a water name like hers, but she didn't pick from the usual classical water lad name stock, maybe because he was a halfling. Therefore, Uncle Tane was not named Prospero, Pericles, or Archimedes, or Irenaeus. With me so far?"

Pip nodded.

"Grandad Pendennis stayed in close touch and had Tam and Tane to visit often, so Tane didn't grow up entirely water-ruled. When he was twenty or so, Tane fell in love with Jillian Jules—a very odd fish, but I like her. Jill has sylvan blood, and the sylvans name their tiddlers with mash-up names. So, for another weird reason, Jill mashed up her name and Tane's—Jillian-Tane and came up with—"

"Jane!"

"Yep. Next one is Sulane . . . Three letters from Jules and three from Tane. Get it?"

"Yes, and Trae—"

"I'm not sure where they were going with that one, unless it's to do with Jill's original surname . . . Freyman . . . or some ancestral thing . . . but Mirri is a mash-up of Grandma and Grandad, and with Tallien they're back to riffing on Tane-Jillian. God alone knows what they'll call the next one. If there is a next one. They're all good kids, though."

"Thank you," Pip said.

Laura grinned at her. "There . . . now you're wishing you hadn't asked."

"Of course I'm not! I wanted to know, and you explained."

"Are we doing practice in the usual place?" Laura went on.

"I thought—the barn."

"Okay. I have a feeling Jane will be along soon, and I can find anyone else we want. Who else *do* we want?"

"Star, maybe?" Pip ventured.

"Star Calder-Quince? I can get her—and maybe a couple of others. Ammie is here somewhere, I think."

"Who's Ammie?"

"Ammie Trip," Laura said. "She's my aunt—my mum's much younger sister. She's not a pro-level dancer, but she'll make a lovely little dancing cat. She's just like one." She paused and pointed off to the side. "She's over there, I think." She took a phone from her pocket and tapped it. "Ammie? Can you come over to the barn, and bring Jane—oh, you've got Jane? Great. See you in a bit. What?" She covered the mouthpiece with her hand. "Am wants to know if you want any tomcats. She's found Tan and Tem loitering and looking lost, and she wants to rescue them."

Pip had a weird feeling of being organised, but time was getting along, so she nodded. "Yes, but—oh, there's a Dad somewhere."

Laura laughed and said, "Lots of them, I should think."

"This one is called Grant. He has marvellous boots."

"I know who you mean." Laura turned slowly and pointed. "Over there, noshing on—no, good God, he's *quaffing*! That had better not be poteen or you won't get any sense out of him for the next three days. I'll get Ammie to rescue him too." She spoke into the phone again then turned to Pip. "Puss in Boots is being parted from his tankard as we speak."

"I think that had better be all—"

Laura held up a thumb, instructed Ammie to bring the two tomcats as well as the one in boots, and hung up.

Pip spotted the herdfee and Mim approaching with Star Calder-Quince.

"We'd best hurry," she said.

Her fear that she'd lose control of another ballet proved unfounded. When everyone convened in the barn, they stood politely, waiting for direction.

Pip looked them over. Apart from Star, Laura, and Jane, and their two musicians, and the somewhat bewildered looking Dad, she had two lanky young men with flopping dark hair and pale complexions. They were so alike they must be brothers and they also bore a strong resemblance to Amalie the dolphin soloist's male partner, Tim. The third stranger was a tiny blonde woman with a round face and the kind of smile that suggested a sweet nature. She was not much taller than Pip. With the tall Laura and men, the medium Jane and Star, and the small Ammie, and ages ranging from Star and the Dad's forty-something to Jane's seventeen, it would be an odd corps de ballet.

But then, Pip thought happily, it *should* be odd. The characters were cats in a dancing class, so *odd* was practically a necessity.

The dancing class was Jane's idea, but Jane seemed happy for Pip to take the lead, so she started as she meant to go on.

First, she smiled at Costas and Mim and directed them to sit on the haybale where Tamzin had sat the day of the sketching. "Can you play us something suitable for ballet exercises, but sort of cattish too?"

Costas grinned and nodded. Mim raised one eyebrow and also her piccolo.

They produced a tangle of music.

Pip was enchanted. It was so obviously right to represent the young cats rushing into the scene because they were late for practice . . .

She held up her hand. "That is the entrance music. Enter from *there* by the door, then settle in front of me. *Reverence*." She cocked her gaze at the two young men. "You tommies know what that means?"

One of them made her a grave curtsy. His brother cuffed him. "Bow, cretin."

They bowed.

"I'm sure you do, Dad."

"Grant," the man said. He produced a flourishing bow worthy of a 17th Century courtier.

Ammie, the blonde, giggled. "I'll do my best."

Jane swept her into a hug.

Laura peeled Jane off.

Star grinned at Pip, adjusted her festival dress, which was styled like Pip's but buttercup yellow and clover green in colour with sparkly gold bits, and said cheerfully, "This is going to be *epic.*"

Chapter Twelve. Talking to Star

Queen of the Clowder, which everyone seemed to call *Cat Ballet,* developed in a lovely chaotic fashion. Pip, as the old queen cat instructing her clowder in proper cat etiquette as well as in dance, had a wonderful time.

The others took it just seriously enough for her to see it coming together.

She was sorry when Jane, who always knew the time, made a lovely *reverence* and ventured, "Miss Pippin, I think you have to be on set in an hour or so. Should we break now?"

Is it that late?

Pip had intended to seek some peace and solitude before returning to Solace's surreal world, but she decided breakfast was a better option.

They say you can rest when you're dead. I shall seek solitude when I'm not at a festival.

She farewelled seven cats and two musicians and had breakfast with Star, who had to be on set when she did.

"Crikey, I knew we'd have a packed schedule, but I didn't know it was going to be *this* packed," Star said, adding pureed fruit to a plate of some sort of pancake. She helped herself to strong Indian tea and topped it up with milk.

Pip availed herself of the pot of cambric tea the blond waiter now brought her as a matter of course.

"I thought you drank camomile," Star said.

"I do, in the cabin or in my flask. I quite like this, too."

Star crinkled her nose. "It's *pallid.* I'm sure I wouldn't."

"All the more for me." Pip recalled something. "Are you

going to give me your contact details so we can plant illicit tulips in honour of Little Mum?"

"Right now. Tell me your number and I'll ring you. You can save me into Contacts."

Pip dug her phone out of her messenger bag and recited her number.

"Better hurry. It's moaning about its battery." She recalled she should have charged it after sliding her feint-lined pad into her messenger bag last night instead of flatlining into bed.

Star called and they saved their contacts. "Grand." Star indicated the promise blank on Pip's wrist. "That's pretty. And interesting. I would have thought you were a cat-person, though."

"I am a cat-person, but I'm getting a puppy soon. I checked in with the cats and they don't mind."

Star, in the middle of a sip of strong tea, choked.

Pip frowned. She'd been feeling comfortable with Star. Star knew of cat ballet, and dancing the full hour, and about pacing oneself, though not being old. She even knew how to give cheek to the playwright and the importance of tulips. Pip had forgotten she wouldn't have heard of fay cats.

She amended her explanation. "Before I came to Delphinium Island I had a holiday—the first one for ten years. I went to a delightful place called the fossmere. That's where I got to know Jane, who is Laura's cousin.

"Laura's brother stayed at my cottage while I was away to look after the cats and the garden. He had his dog with him, and the cats got along with it surprisingly well."

"What sort of dog?" Star asked with apparent interest.

"He looks like a chocolate poodle," Pip said with truth and evasion. "His name is Kakao, which means—"

"Chocolate. Are you getting a chocolate poodle?"

"No—mine's a medium-sized breed I'd never heard of

until recently."

"A designer dog?"

"I think it's more of a *regional* breed. Someone else is organising it for me, but I know he will be black and reasonably quiet. I'm going to call him Tektite."

"Interesting. What are your cats' names? What are they like?"

"They're not exactly *my* cats. They just choose to live with me. Kittisack looks like a Siamese. He's secretive and superior. Amberjill is a calico. She's quite elusive but mostly sweet. The third one is Lupin's cat."

"Oh?"

"He's made of pottery and painted with lupins. He's a kind of household guardian. My cousin made him."

"Aha." Star pounced. "So you, too, have peculiar cousins."

"Not many of them now," Pip said sadly. She drained her tea and picked up another fruit bun with a lode of cream cheese running through it and flecks of golden flower petals in among the currants. She thought she probably needed her strength.

Star drained her cup too. "Off to the salt mines . . . or in my case, to a hospital bed." She patted her cheeks. "Do I have a healthy glow?"

"Yes," Pip said honestly. She bit her bun.

"Dammit, that means more makeup from Ward's powder-puff minions. Did you know he has *five* of them now? I think they're breeding in a cupboard under the stairs. One of the new ones suggested I needed to stay out of the sun and to cultivate a sad pallor. After all, Perdita has been lying in that room for years. *I* said I had my Caraway's Comfort Loving Lotion, and *he* said—"

"SPF-forty," Pip said sadly. She humped her knees under her skirt.

"How did you guess?"

"I know the one you mean. He said it to me, too. You won't remember this, but when *I* was a wee thing—"

"Wee-er than now?"

Pip lobbed a stray currant at Star. "When *I* was a wee-er-than-now thing, back in the fifties, sunlight was good for us. It gave us a rosy glow. Little Mum used to take me out in the garden and lay me out on a blanket while she planted stuff. She was hardening me off along with the tomato plants. It was considered wise, not eccentric, and *certainly* not abusive."

Star said, "I think I remember just the edge of that time . . . not the fifties, of course, but before we were all terrified of the sun. We knew sunburn hurt, but we also knew tan was *protective.*" She frowned. "It's disconcerting when things we *know* get arbitrarily rug-jerked."

Pip nodded emphatic agreement. "It's difficult not to dislike the rug-jerkers. I always get the urge to—"

"Shoot the messenger," Star broke in.

"Exactly. But if *I* had a Perdita in my life, I wouldn't just let her lie there. Not that I'd let her get sunburned, but I'd take her out for a bed-ride, somewhere nice."

"Such as the top of a hill, and scoot her down like a shopping trolley?" Star suggested.

"Maybe not that. Mind, I remember in a book someone called for *hush* because a character was unconscious. I wondered *why*. She couldn't hear and be disturbed, and didn't they want her to wake up?"

"That was the total point of a story called *Trapdoor*. There was a boy who had been in a coma for years, and some visiting children found him and didn't keep their voices down and he started to wake up."

"What was his name?" Pip asked with interest.

"I don't remember. I don't think he had one." Star rocked back, as if preparing to get up. Then she said, "I wonder if we *could* do something like that. Not make a noise, but the bed-ride idea. Humph and Jasper didn't jump on you when you appropriated Mother's sweater."

So Star *had* noticed that.

"No-o—but rescuing a sweater that was sliding off her lap is a bit different from unhitching someone from a lot of machinery and running off with her."

"Not that much machinery," Star objected. "They went the minimalistic route. I'm supposed to be the sleeping beauty, not the bride of Frankenstein with tubes and metal stuck to me. And listen—if Solace *did* take Perdida for a recreational spin, the machines wouldn't matter."

"Why not?"

Star waved her hands airily. "Because Solace isn't bound by human rules. She could take Perdita out for a midnight adventure, and no one would ever know. Mind you—the director might go ape-shit. He's a bit out of his comfort zone already, poor love."

"Humph might be cross too," Pip said. "Anyway, we can't do it. Solace doesn't have any validity outside the hospital room until the very last scene, when Perdita wakes and Solace leaves the building."

"Dammit. I'd forgotten that." Star frowned, spinning her wedding ring. "But listen . . . *why* has Solace no validity beyond the room? Is it an immutable law, or is she tied to Perdita? Because if she's tied to Perdita, she *could* go out, if she took Perdita with her."

"I sort of see what you mean, but I think if we went as far off-piste as that, Stew would stop filming. We'd be leaving the set, and he wouldn't know what was going on."

"Maybe Solace could suggest it though . . . talk it through with Perdita and talk herself out of it. Isn't part of her personality agoraphobic? Or maybe *shut in*?"

Pip saw that Star was right. "We could try. Maybe in one of the later scenes, when the visits are drying up. It would be in the spirit of what Humph intended . . ."

Star nodded enthusiastically. "You could make it a truly heartfelt monologue! There wouldn't be a dry eye in the house. By the way, Pip, what you said regarding the ending made me think. I know Humph left it open and up to you how you leave the room. He left it up to me how Perdita wakes, too. Whether I look vaguely around or wake and start crying when I see my so-aged reflection, or even sit bolt upright with staring eyes. But what about Solace?"

What *about* Solace, Pip wondered.

"I don't know."

"I thought you always knew?"

"So did I. Maybe I'll know when I come to do it."

Star said, "Maybe we both will. Pip—what's been your favourite role over the years? I've been mainly in plays and a few small mumsy parts in soaps. They blur together, but your roles have been—um—"

Eccentric? Eclectic? Odd? Quaint?

"I loved being Marigold Heriot," Pip said without hesitation.

"Why in particular? If it's not a rude question."

"I got to be carried off on a horse by a highwayman."

"I guess that would be fun. I chickened out of performing the stunt in Humph's prologue, but that wasn't *riding,* it was *falling.* And as I said, if I damaged myself it would be inconvenient all round."

"I was scared of my stunt too, and I didn't even have to fall," Pip said, thinking back. "Sully—my agent back then—said it was my choice, and Alain said he'd make sure I was all right, so I said *yes.*"

"Obviously it *was* all right, since you enjoyed yourself," Star said.

"It was *magical.*" Pip recalled the hoofbeats and the sudden ensuing silence. She remembered the starstruck days of filming, time in the green room where Alain played his lute and talked to her as if she was his friend rather than the Tiny Pippin Pearmain who was gifted seed-pearl bracelets and plush cats with diamanté collars by the studio. He'd addressed her as Pipkin, which might have felt demeaning but which she'd liked. It was a diminutive of sorts, she supposed, but the k sound made it distinguished. They're played several scenes together. They'd also gone exploring around the grounds of Oakengrove and fossicked on the nearby beach, but riding Varian in Alain's arms had been the high point.

Star cleared her throat. "I do admit to replaying that gallop-away scene on video and daydreaming of being Marigold, especially when the shawl blew loose, and the highwayman snatched it out of the air without even looking. Then, when you were back on the ground, he tucked it around your shoulders. He looked down and you looked up and it was just as if you were alone with no cameras or lights or director. It was so *real.* It was more intimate than if you'd gone for a big theatrical embrace. That scene was one of the things that pushed me into acting and made me understand it had to be real, and true. Alain Barfleur was so different from the general seventies and eighties stars with the bell-bottoms or big hair. He was beautiful—my first big crush. I wonder whatever happened to him. He should have gone on to be as big as Sir Harrison Arthur."

"I was in a film with him."

"Who—Sir Harrison?"

"Yes. Only he wasn't a sir then. He played a Victorian explorer who caused a fuss when he went into society to find a wife."

"I'm guessing you weren't the wife."

"No. I was an urchin called Carlotta Monello he'd collected on his travels. He dressed me up and pretended I was his little sister Charlotte. I was seventeen or so but playing eleven. His mistress—an opera singer played by a woman who was his real-life wife—outed him by declaring he didn't have a sister. There was a lot of drama, and Dominique Fortesque—the singer—milked it for all she was worth."

"I don't remember that one."

"No one does. It was a lot of fun to do, but it was one of his rare box office failures. *A Fig for Ferdinand,* it was called. As for what happened to Alain, I don't know." Pip ate the last of her bun, let her knees out from under her skirt and rotated her ankles. She confessed, "I was quite thrilled when Sully said I was up for a role in *Pageant Spectacular* and that Alain was already cast as the Silver Knight. That was in 1982."

"I don't think I know that one, either. You got the part?"

"I did. It was slated as a grand celebration of the Golden Age of the Silver Screen, but there was some kind of legal challenge the studio wasn't expecting. The original idea was to recreate iconic scenes and characters from Golden Age films, but the rights and concepts were owned by various people and organisations, and the licensing fees turned out to be astronomical, so in the end, they created their own iconic characters and filmed them *as if* they were famous. Sort of parallel worlding. Or you might call it a tongue-in-cheek production . . . sort of mockumentary, though I don't think they used that term back then."

"How—bizarre!" Star said, laughing.

"That's exactly what it was! I think a few people believed the characters *had* been icons and that they'd just happened to miss them. Cue a lot of searching through film libraries and books of forgotten movies. Alain was the Silver Knight, a kind of Galahad figure, who woke in a stone circle and came clank-jingling into town thee-ing and thou-ing and prithee-ing."

"Did you get to be carried off again? Or rescued from a dragon?"

"No." Pip still felt the sting of disappointment after all these years. She had built a lot on that role, and all the stars seemed to align—only for them to fizzle out, much as the much-anticipated sighting of Halley's Comet had fizzled a few years later.

"Oh. What part did you play in this weird mash-up?"

"I was a character called—wait for it—Teacup Beloved. It was a kind of faux-fairy tale, with a touch of the Baroque period. Sully said they were riffing on *Thumbelina* and *The Little Mermaid* and *Neverland* and *Alice* and God knows what else. They might even have been inspired by those teacup dogs."

"I'm surprised I missed that one," Star said. "It sounds mad enough to be in my top twenty. I *love* those would-be-cult films no one has ever heard of. My favourite is a choice little number from the late 1920s, called *Madam Sin,* starring a lady pirate." She rubbed her hands like a pantomime villain. "You *should* see the rah-rah advertising! I have an actual poster of Madam staring out from under her hat with a *dare you* expression. The actress was called Lass Schubert. Remind me to show you sometime." She paused. "But you were saying?"

"Nearly everyone missed the Spectacular," Pip said. "The ones who did see it probably felt undereducated because they didn't recognise the so-called *iconic characters* or else duped because they knew they were ersatz and suspected they were being led up the garden path. Anyway, I didn't get carried off on a horse. I pirouetted and twittered. I didn't see Alain and Varian at all. His last day of filming was the day before my first, and he had to hurry off."

She shrugged. "Still, I got a souvenir."

Oops. That slipped out.

Star chuckled. "Don't tell me you're one of those actors who steal those white towelling dressing gowns, or coasters, or make off with the paper-mache dragon-head props."

"Not likely—" Pip broke off as a pair of menacing shoes appeared in front of her lowered gaze. They weren't Jane's soft slippers, or Tamzin's beautiful rainbow-heeled sandals, or the blond waiter's prosaic running shoes, or Grant's impressive steel-capped boots, or even the Tyrolean shoes Yanick the baker wore under his lederhosen. They were sturdy brogues, polished to a terrifying face-reflecting sheen. They belonged to Magda Saxer.

Chapter Thirteen. In a Strop

Pip gave a guilty start.

Star cast her gaze down, biting her lip.

Magda said, "I thought you were a professional."

Her cold words were directed at Pip, but Star said, "She is."

"Being late on set is as unprofessional as it's possible to be, aside from being late *and* incapable on set," Magda snapped.

"Sorry," Pip offered. She really was. She'd never been incapable on set, if Magda meant drunk, but she thought it better not to say so. She had almost never been late, either.

"I'm a bad influence," Star remarked. She sounded contrite, but there was an edge of flippancy in her voice.

Magda turned cold eyes on the Biblio-Rep woman. "You might well be a bad influence, but Pippin is an adult and it's up to her not to be influenced by you or by anyone else."

"We were talking," Pip said.

"Considering your much-vaunted reclusiveness, that's—" Magda stopped short. She passed her hand over her thick white hair, patting her braid into place. "I'm too old for this."

Star straightened from her half-reclining position. Her flippancy was gone, and she looked troubled. "Missus Saxer, we are truly sorry. I know we're here to work, but I'm afraid I'm also treating it as a bit of a break from the everyday concerns. We have a packed schedule, and we came straight from a dance rehearsal to breakfast. We tend to take a few minutes to unwind whenever we can get them."

Magda appeared unmollified. "You're not my concern here. You are free to do as you like because it won't reflect on me. However—" She jabbed Pip with a glare. "You told me you understood why you are here—to make a film. *Not* to dance, or to play, or to *unwind*—"

Star got up, and Pip saw, fascinated, that her smooth cheeks were turning dull red. She was as tall as Magda, and she looked the agent in the eyes. "Missus Saxer, we have apologised. Time got away from us, but we weren't *playing,* as you put it. We were talking about our roles. We are portraying two aspects of the same character, so it makes sense to do some teamwork. We were discussing one of Pip's improv scenes. We also went into the end scene, which Humph and the director have left largely up to us to develop in partnership.

"What we each choose to do will go some way to informing what the other does. That said, we should have been more careful of keeping aware of the time. I'll set my alarm from now on, but perhaps today someone might have called us rather than sending you to play sheepdog?"

"No one sent me, and I called Pippin three times," Magda said.

Pip glanced at her messenger bag before belatedly remembering the state of her phone battery.

"My phone's flat," she said, thumbing it on. She held it out like Exhibit A in a murder trial, watching as it booted up, flashed its screen like an ingenue's eyes, beeped once and subsided into its coma.

Pip did it again. The phone did it again.

"Dead as a nit," Pip said mournfully.

"Good," Magda said.

Star raised an eyebrow. "Mine's not dead. And why *good*?"

"Because if it wasn't, she might have thought I was wilfully ignoring her, or had put her on silent, and that would have been unforgivable," Pip said.

"I didn't have *your* number," Magda said pointedly to Star.

"Humph has," Star said. "So have the other bibs. Any of

them would have given it to you, or made the call themselves, if you'd asked."

Magda ignored that. "If you hurry we might just make it." She turned and strode away.

Star pursed her lips in a silent whistle. "Holy canary! She's in a strop."

"She has a right to be," Pip said.

"Perhaps so, but she doesn't have the right to tear strips off you in front of me. It's damned bad manners." Star pulled her phone out of her pocket and woke it up. "Humph sent me an email. An *email!* Has the man never heard of actually *ringing*? Or even texting?"

She quickly dialled a number as she walked. "Humph? It's Star. We're coming. Got caught in conversational traffic. With you in five."

Pip, trotting along in double time to keep up with Star's long strides, felt ridiculous and sheepish. She supposed it was good of Star to be in her corner against Magda, but she was utterly able to defend herself at need. The fact that she hadn't was because she *had* been in the wrong. She should have been aware of the time, and she should have charged her phone.

She had done neither. She had poor time-sense, but she'd been aware of that since childhood, and she mostly took steps to make sure it didn't inconvenience other people. This time she'd dropped the ball. There was no defending the indefensible.

No wonder Magda was annoyed. She had been peevish, and Pip thought that was probably her fault as well. Magda would no doubt realise, as Star had said, that she should have kept her comments for a more private moment.

Sully wouldn't have. She'd have told me off as and when she thought it was necessary, but I never gave her much trouble.

No time to make things right now, she decided. She'd have to get today's filming done with her usual efficiency. She would charge her phone in the first break and keep her time-sense under control, as much as she could. Maybe a written schedule would be helpful. Since moving to Jellico Bay, she'd hardly ever had to bother about other people's schedules. She had her tart order each Thursday, but she could pick those up any time, and her only regular visitor had been Mister Clancy. Aside from keeping in a store of Bushman's Best and some strong Indian tea, she hadn't needed to make any special preparations for him. He just turned up and tapped on the door whenever he felt like conversation and company. Since his passing into glory, she'd missed his wide-ranging conversation. That was another reason she'd been so engrossed with talking to Star.

A schedule was necessary now. Not only would it mollify Magda and keep Pip's professional reputation intact, but it would mean she could avoid causing anxiety or anger in anyone else.

With a new list to prepare in any spare moments offered, Pip began her happy mosquito hum.

Chapter Fourteen. Downtrodden Tabby

After all that fuss about their supposed lateness from Magda, Pip was both relieved and mildly miffed to discover there was plenty of time.

Jasper and Stew had set up a monitor to play through the rushes—the scenes they had already in the can. Most of the day's cast lounged around, peering over shoulders, or streaming the password-protected video on their own phones, looking pleased, chagrined, or puzzled as they took in their own performances and, peripherally, someone else's.

Rushes were often confusing, but because *Half-Life of the Lost* was being filmed as a play, and thus more or less in scene order and also with the lighting and much of the sound already in place, the material they watched was much closer to the finished film than was usual.

Another camera operator . . . the blonde Allirra Diamond, whom Pip had seen briefly at the studio, was filming the actors watching the rushes.

Someone else—good God, it was Humph! was filming Allirra filming the—

Pip lost track of her thoughts as her day plunged even more deeply into the surreal.

Ward spotted her and beckoned imperiously. "Call off the womanhunt! Kennel the bloodhounds! Cease the seers! Preempt the prayers! The lost sheep have been found!" he proclaimed, waving his Rembrandt hat.

"Pack it in, Ward, we were just a bit delayed, and nobody even has the tenterhooks out," Star said. She gestured towards the activity. "Not that it seems anyone is remotely ready for us anyway."

"Nevertheless, my darlings, ready or not, you have a date with the powder monkeys," Ward said. He extracted two minions from the crowd and thrust Star and Pip in their directions. "Darlings, two sacrificial lambs to conduct for the slaughter."

Star, perhaps not liking to be chivvied, made her own way to the screened off area which served as the makeup room. She got into the chair and relaxed while Pip, as usual, eyed the step up into her own chair. She was agile, but the step was quite high for someone of shorter stature. She lifted one foot, and her chin almost came in contact with her knee. She was reminded of setting her foot in a stirrup.

"Do you need any help, Miss Pearmain?"

Pip looked behind her, into the anxious blue eyes of a very young minion with cropped blonde hair. About to say something sharp, she restrained herself and smiled instead. "No thanks, I can manage. I just need a moment to steel myself for the effort." She got a better grip on the chair and made it into the seat. Maybe it wasn't much like a stirrup after all. At least the makeup chair didn't sidle off to snatch a mouthful of grass.

The minion wrapped her in a soft pink cape and applied a cotton mobcap. "There is a pedal to lower the chair if you prefer," she said in a low tone.

"I can manage, but thank you for telling me." Pip, glancing over the minion's shoulder, encountered a camera lens. She smiled and waggled her fingers at the operator. "Allirra Diamond, right? I had marigold tea with your mum a few days ago and I saw you in transit."

"So I heard." Allirra stuck her thumb up the way Stew did.

"Don't mind me. Consider me a bee on a wall."

The minion looked uneasy.

"Not fond of flies," Allirra explained.

"You can go ahead now," Pip said, overriding any possible etymological digressions.

The minion blurted, "I'm just the—"

Pip cut her off. "You're not *just* anything. And you don't need to take my makeup off because I'm not wearing any. Just run over my face with a wet-wipe. Then rub in a pea-sized dot of Caraway's Kissed by Dew." She closed her eyes and shortly felt a tentative dabbing, followed by the gentle glide and subtle scent of the face-cream she'd used since childhood.

"Okay, now you use Stage Shades Number Six with a slightly damp sponge . . . use a new one. Rinse it and it can dry out between scenes." She waited a few beats as the minion hesitated.

"Um . . . it might say *Nuances de Scène* on the tub. I'm used to the English version, but I think French Canadia . . . um—I think the company was bought out so someone else who translated the name into French."

The minion pounced.

Pip said, "Down the centreline, blend it outwards and down my neck." She lay back and hummed . . . not the high mosquito, but the softer sound made up of music from *Queen of the Clowder*.

"That's a cool tune," the minion said, still dabbing away tentatively.

"It's the tommies' interval wash routine," Pip said in her ventriloquist's voice. It was surprising how the tricks of the trade came back to her. Being able to speak without moving her lips meant she could converse with makeup artists without interrupting their work. She'd played a ventriloquist in *Medium Rare* and also in *Me and Miss Moody*.

"Oh, is that from Cat Ballet?" the minion asked.

Queen of the Clowder, Pip objected mentally, but she said, "Yes. How did you know?"

"Ummm . . ."

"I suppose you're friends with one of my dancers," Pip said, in case she'd sounded sharp or accusing. She thought the minion was just a bit younger than Jane, but less self-confident. Jane was pretty much unsquashable.

"S-sort of."

The minion wiped over the blended makeup with a clean cloth.

"You can put a bit of Macro Six on my cheekbones," Pip said. "The effect should be ethereal and a bit surreal, but not full-blown corpse bride or death warmed over. Don't want to scare the camerapeople."

The minion fumbled around and Allirra Diamond, evidently an efficient young woman, used a spare finger to indicate the *Mergé Macro Bâtons* in their case.

"Thanks." The minion investigated.

Pip felt the soft touches along her cheekbones as the girl—she must stop thinking of her as a minion—measured the distance. She really was green. The experienced makeup artists could hit the cheekbone with their eyes shut. Maybe they played *pin the blush on the cheekbone* in whatever they used as a green room until they had it down pat.

"That's it," Pip said, opening her eyes.

The girl was staring at her with eyes the deep blue of cornflowers. If not for the scared rabbit expression, she would have been beautiful in a gamine fashion.

Now what?

Pip sighed. "Listen . . . what's your name?"

"Candlemas," the girl said in a resigned tone.

"Oh, nice! Candlemas, I can see you want to know something or other, but you're going to have to ask me whatever it is directly. I'm not intuitive."

A faint snort from the camerawoman annoyed her.

"I'm *not.* Maybe with performing I am, but not otherwise." She turned her attention back to the makeup artist. "So, Candlemas, what do you want to know?"

The girl put aside her sponge and removed the cap from Pip's hair, doing it gently so as not to pull. She was unravelling the cape when another minion came in. "Right, let's get you—" He stared at Pip. She stared back.

"Already taken care of," she said.

"By whom?"

So, he was an *educated* minion. He got the objective pronoun right.

"One of the other artists came in before you," Pip said airily. She smiled at Candlemas. "Thanks for helping me off with this. I got straitjacketed and I didn't want to smudge myself."

The educated minion nodded in a lordly way, said, "You may sweep up in here," to Candlemas, and went out.

The snout of the camera followed his retreat, then Allirra Diamond turned it off. "He'll know the truth when the doco comes out."

"Not if you don't use that bit of footage," Pip said.

"It's gold."

"It won't matter to me by then," Candlemas pointed out. "I'll be long gone."

"Atta girl." Allirra went out.

Pip slid down from the chair, bending her knees to absorb the shock.

Behind her, Star and her own minion choked with laughter.

Pip said, "Ja. *Und*?"

Candlemas said in a hurry, "I wanted to ask if you could fit another cat in your ballet. I do a very decent downtrodden tabby."

"Can you dance?" Pip asked.

The girl wrapped her arms around herself, puffed her

cheeks slightly, and danced a little sketch.

A loud hiss and spit sound from behind them made Pip glance at Star, who was just returning her face to normal.

Candlemas cringed and fell over her paws then retreated, turning back to glare briefly and switch a non-existent tail.

Pip said, "You're in. Seven in the morning at the barn."

The girl raised a thumb in acknowledgment and slunk out, hips swinging and tail waving.

CHAPTER FIFTEEN. DEMI-POINTE

"Not bad, if I do say it myself," Star said, squirming out of her makeup cape with her healthy glow replaced by Perdita's serene pallor. She smiled her thanks at her makeup artist who was leaving to deal with someone else. "You won't feel the need to mention anything you happened to overhear?" she asked gently.

He gestured at his earbuds and mouthed, *eh?*

Star gave him a cheerful nod.

"At makeup or dance?" Pip asked, admiring Star's assured dismissal.

"Both. She's a quick study with natural talents in both. Not that she's qualified in either."

Pip frowned. "How do you know?"

Star said, "I ought to know, and I can also claim credit, up to a point. I'm her mother."

"I see. So, you told her about *Queen of the Clowder*?"

Star stretched to hold her calves. "I did not," she said from down by her ankles. "Ugh. I wish my back would flex more." She added, reasonably, "How could I have told her? I didn't *know* anything regarding Cat Ballet until Mim and Costas found me and suggested I might join in. I've been with you ever since then, getting you into trouble with your agent."

"Sorry for implying you'd been blabbing. Not that it would have mattered a fig if you had. *Queen of the Clowder* is not exactly a state secret."

"No need to be sorry." Star stretched upwards and arched her back. "It was a logical assumption. For the record, I don't know how my kid found out, unless it was by teen-osmosis. She's pretty good at that."

"She's pretty good at interpretive dance, too, from what I saw. Why hasn't she joined us on other mornings?"

"She only got here late last night," Star said. "Somewhat traumatised by Mister Handsome on the boom-gate, I think."

Pip frowned. Mull St Ives had given Matin the run-around, but evidently that was just a bit of family aggro. Surely he wouldn't be unkind to an innocent young woman like Candlemas Calder-Quince.

Candlemas Calder-Quince! That's a name and a half to live up to. Wonder what her second name is.

She asked.

"Caraway," Star said.

Pip said, politely, "You named your kid after your favourite cosmetics line?"

Star fell into a relaxed posture. "As you might say, *Ja. Und?* Anyway, I don't class Caraway's Comforts as cosmetics, per se. They're . . ." She moved her hand in circles.

"Comforts?" Pip suggested.

"*Essentials,*" Star asserted. "One-stop-shop. I even use the toothpowder."

"Really?"

"Indeed. It's the best there is! All natural, and at *such* a moderate price," Star added, striking an attitude. She continued, dead-pan, "Buy now! Buy today! Accept no substitutes!"

Pip stared at her in wonder. "Are you feeling quite all right?"

"Yes. Sorrow." Star grinned at her. "My inner self-interest took possession of me."

Pip went on staring, sure that would elicit added information.

Star stared back for a few seconds. Then she sighed. "Okay . . . Pippin Pearmain, how does anyone know what you're thinking? You don't have tells . . . unless one counts the humming, and that seems to mean more than one possibility."

Pip said, "My cousin Jan said something like that. The answer is this—the easiest way to know what I'm thinking is to ask me. Otherwise, you might just come out and tell me what you're hinting at instead of dancing about the bushes."

Star's eyes widened.

"Sorry if that offended you." Pip really was sorry. She liked Star. Aside from her occasional surges of warmth towards Jan and Clarkia, and her shared love of dancing with Jane, she felt closer to Star than to anyone else in a long time.

I'll miss her when I go home.

Nonsense. It's a holiday womance.

Star said, "No apologies needed. I was trailing a lure and you were quite right to call me on it. I'll give you the facts and a disclaimer. I *do* love and use the Caraway's Comforts brand almost exclusively for all my skincare needs. I believe it lives up to its mission statement—that the foundation of health and beauty is more important than the icing, just as the contents are more important than the packaging. Most of the ingredients are eatable or at the very least, harmless if accidently ingested."

"And?" Pip urged when Star fell silent.

"*And,* the company belongs to the family," Star said. "It's certainly not mine exclusively, but I, and the kids, come to that, get a dividend most years. We're not obliged to use the products, but we do—because they darned well work as advertised."

"I know they do," Pip said. "Little Mum and Little Nanna Laurel always used them and so do I. They smell good, too." She fixed Star with a sharp gaze. "Come clean. What *is* that scent? The packaging says *At Caraway's, we use a secret blend of tinctures and oils from an old-fashioned garden . . .* and that's not exactly informative. I suspect there's some violet and rose in there and possibly honeysuckle and cucumber, but what else?"

Star shrugged expressively. "I can't tell you. And I mean *can't,* not *won't.* I don't know the exact blend . . . I don't make it personally, you see. Obviously, I know some of the plants growing in the Caraway Secret Gardens, and yes, there are roses and sweet violets, but I don't know the details of what goes into what, let alone the proportions." Her expression turned briefly sorrowful. "When Mum goes to glory, as you so nicely put it, I inherit both her place in the firm *and* access to the original book of recipes, not to say a learning curve so steep it will look like the foothills of Mount O'Connor. You may be sure that, curious as I may be, I'm in no hurry for that to happen."

"Of course not." Pip felt a renewed stab of sorrow for Little Mum who had *not* been the CEO or Creative Force or Lord High Chemist or whatever of a boutique company, but who had loved her life among the flowers and trees of her garden.

I should have stayed at Treasures to look after her garden . . .

But then you would not have had Lemonwood Cottage. Then, you would not have had us.

Pip froze.

K-Kittisack? She had just enough presence of mind to make it a silent enquiry.

She expected silence, or a cattish snigger. What she got was an oddly gentle comment.

I am always with you, Pippin Pearmain.

It could have been creepy and stalkerish but oddly enough—it wasn't.

Star seemed to contemplate saying something more, but at that point, a minion—not Candlemas—poked his head in and suggested Solace and Perdita were wanted onstage pronto. Or else. He didn't actively voice the last two words, but that *was* the connotation.

"Eek," Star said, *sotto voce*. "We're not in costume. Pippin Pearmain, you are such a terribly bad influence on me. I pride myself on slithering enigmatically through life without causing ripples, but for some reason *you* make me garrulous, neglectful, and refocused.

"There in three," she told the minion.

He started to argue, but Star began peeling off her yellow and green dress and as a pair of serviceable waist-high knickers came into view, he scarpered.

Star gave Pip a wink. "Nothing like a disrobing middle-aged woman to terrify a little male minion." She stretched and tossed her dress over a chair. As she scrambled into Perdita's nightie *de jure,* Pip was disappointed to see that her friend favoured not only sensible solid knickers but a seamless T-shirt bra in a depressing shade of beige.

How odd. How ordinary. How boring.

"I'm off to coma-land," Star said, scooting out the door with the words trailing behind her in an almost visible stream.

Just like a parlourmaid's ribbons, Pip thought. She'd never seen a parlourmaid, but she'd been one in a play called *Duchess Undone.*

Pip found herself assuming the high-nosed air she'd worn as the redoubtable Pastinaken, whose name was funny only if one knew it meant Parsnip in German . . .and not very, even then. She shook off the shadow of that old role, tilted her nose back to its usual angle and hurriedly peeled herself out of her dress. She briefly admired her green wispy knickers and matching lace bra before she hauled on a shirt, which was carnation pink today, and stepped into her overalls.

Ouch! She just managed not to squawk aloud as the clip of her bib-and-brace overalls caught the flesh of her finger as she did it up.

Must you? she demanded of the universe. *I just thought her underwear was boring and mine is so much nicer. I didn't say it aloud! Maybe I ought to direct her to the Wispy Knickers website so she can pick up something more becoming.*

Or maybe not. How much would *she* resent it if someone

tried to get *her* to wear something serviceable and seamless?

Mind you, she couldn't imagine anyone trying. No one, except possibly Jisinia, had ever exhibited an interest in Pip's underpinnings since the long-ago days when she'd taken advice from the little ladies in her family.

Wear nice knickers. Even if no one sees them, you'll know they are there. At the first hint of sagging or bagging, retire them. Cut them into strips and make rag mats—she never had—*or discreet ties for staking in the garden*. She'd done that.

Halfway across the set, she was still adjusting the second overall strap and realising she'd forgotten to put on her shoes.

Never mind.

Pip rose on demi-pointe and danced across the stage.

Perdita lay motionless in her serene otherwhere, breathing gently. Pip felt Solace at her shoulder, restless, enquiring—real. She hitched herself up onto the bed, reached out and patted Perdita's face with three fingertips.

"Wake up! Let's dance!"

She stretched out her legs, tilted her feet and waggled her toes before sliding down to land light as a moth on the hospital linoleum that was suggested by lighting but not entirely there.

"Never mind, Perdita. *I'll* dance anyway. *You* can dance in your mind, okay? Maybe one day your feet will follow."

She swung into an arabesque and froze as the door opened and a nurse came in carrying a clipboard.

"Dance in your mind," Solace said to the nurse. "If you can't dance through life en pointe, you can always try demi-pointe."

The nurse checked Perdita's vitals.

Solace danced on demi-pointe, clad in her overalls, her carnation-pink shirt . . . and lacy green knickers unseen.

About the Author

Lark Westerly loves writing series where characters weave in and out of one another's stories.

She also loves playing with ideas and notions and researching odd information.

Lark lives in the island state of Tasmania, where she walks dogs, invents recipes, and goes around in clothes with that lived-in look. She rarely finds a matching pair of socks.

Unlike Pippin Pearmain, Lark is not tiny, not an only child, not single, and not an on-screen performer. She never learned ballet and she can't speak Cat-Morse. She doesn't even have a bucket list. Nevertheless, Pippin Pearmain and Lark Westerly are sisters under the skin.

Oh . . . you were wondering about that bucket that inspired *Performing Pippin Pearmain*? It happened like this . . .

To find out, visit

https://performingpippinpearmain.weebly.com/about-the-bucket.html

www.ingramcontent.com/pod-product-compliance
Lightning Source LLC
LaVergne TN
LVHW020641100826
845148LV00012B/2276

* 9 7 8 1 4 8 7 4 3 7 1 9 0 *